Fabulous Fathers

"Would you mind if I conducted a little experiment?"

Joshua murmured.

"An experiment?" Cassie's voice seemed thin and far off.

"You see, I came up with an hypothesis that kissing you would expel you from my mind." He chuckled, a throaty, sexy sound. "I don't believe it will work," he admitted huskily, "but I *am* a scientist. And proving and disproving theories is my life."

She closed her eyes and his palm cupped her jaw.

"So what do you say?" he whispered. "May I kiss you?"

Dear Reader,

This month we have a terrific lineup of stories, guaranteed to warm you on these last chilly days of winter. March comes in like a lion with a great new FABULOUS FATHER by Donna Clayton. Joshua Kingston may have learned a thing or two about child-rearing from his son's new nanny, Cassie Simmons. But now the handsome professor wants to teach Cassie a few things about love! The *Nanny and the Professor* is sure to touch your heart.

Elizabeth August concludes her WHERE THE HEART IS series with *A Husband for Sarah*. You've watched Sarah Orman in previous titles bring couples together. Now Sarah gets a romance—and a wedding—all her own!

A *Wife Most Unlikely* is what Laney Fulbright is to her best friend, Jack Austin. But Laney's the only woman this sexy bachelor wants! Linda Varner brings MR. RIGHT, INC. to a heartwarming conclusion.

Alaina Hawthorne brings us two people who strike a marriage bargain in *My Dearly Beloved*. Vivian Leiber tells an emotional story of a police officer and the woman he longs to love and protect in *Safety of His Arms*. And this month's debut author, Dana Lindsey, brings us a handsome, lonely widower and the single mom who's out to win his heart in *Julie's Garden*.

In the coming months, look for books by favorite authors Suzanne Carey, Marie Ferrarella, Diana Palmer and many others.

Happy reading!

Anne Canadeo
Senior Editor
Silhouette Romance

Please address questions and book requests to:
Silhouette Reader Service
U.S.: 3010 Walden Ave., P.O. Box 1325, Buffalo, NY 14269
Canadian: P.O. Box 609, Fort Erie, Ont. L2A 5X3

NANNY AND THE PROFESSOR

Donna Clayton

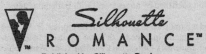

Silhouette
ROMANCE™
Published by Silhouette Books
America's Publisher of Contemporary Romance

For Janice
Judging my life from the friendships I share,
yours alone makes me the richest woman on earth

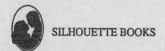 SILHOUETTE BOOKS

ISBN 0-373-19066-2

NANNY AND THE PROFESSOR

Copyright © 1995 by Donna Fasano

This edition published by arrangement with Harlequin Enterprises B.V.

Printed in U.S.A.

Books by Donna Clayton

Silhouette Romance

Mountain Laurel #720
Taking Love in Stride #781
Return of the Runaway Bride #999
Wife for a While #1039
Nanny and the Professor #1066

DONNA CLAYTON

spent her youth visiting a multitude of imaginary places with the help of scores of wonderful books. Her joy in reading turned into a joy of writing. Now she spends her days creating her own imaginary places and bringing to life characters she hopes her readers will come to love.

Living in Newark, Delaware, with her husband and two sons, Donna thoroughly enjoys the time they spend hiking, skiing and watching old movies together. She still delights in her love of reading and has gladly passed this entertaining addiction to her children. Donna also collects cookbooks, old and new, and even uses them now and then.

Joshua Kingston on Fatherhood...

My Dearest Andrew,

There aren't words to describe the love and
overwhelming joy I felt the first time I held you in
my arms. When your tiny fingers closed around my
thumb, a lump rose in my throat and I wanted to
shout, "Look, world, my perfect son!" I saw your
thatch of red hair, your soft, rosy skin and your big,
dark eyes—so like my own—and I was overcome
with a fierce determination to protect you from
harm, no matter what. I've tried hard to do just that.

But now you're older and our relationship is
changing. You're drawing away from me and I can't
seem to do anything right. My instinct to protect
you causes an awkwardness between us that was
never there before. Give me a complicated scientific
equation to solve and I'll be fine, but to know that I
no longer successfully fulfill my role as your father
is very frustrating. Don't worry though, son, help is
close at hand.

Until then, though, how about having a little
patience with me? I'm smart, but I never professed
to know it all. And remember, you'll always have
my love.

Dad

Chapter One

Cassie Simmons parked her car in front of the impressive stone Tudor-style home and rechecked the house number carefully. In the hopes of calming her jittery nerves she smoothed her hand against her tense abdomen, closed her eyes and inhaled deeply several times. Mary Kingston, Cassie's landlady, had claimed that her nephew was desperate for a live-in nanny. Cassie hoped it was true—because she was desperate for a job.

She turned off the ignition and fixed her anxious gaze on the big house that sat back some distance from the road. The butterflies in her stomach were having a grand old time dancing a jig to the music her apprehension provided.

Mrs. Kingston had said that the nanny position came with room and board, that the salary was generous. Of course, Mary could sometimes become a little absentminded, but if the lovable lady's information was correct, this job was a perfect solution to Cassie's predicament. Cassie only hoped she could make Professor Joshua Kingston understand about Eric and that she *had* to have him with her.

As she thought of the impending interview with Joshua Kingston, her hands trembled. Because he was a college professor, an intelligent and scholarly man, Cassie knew she'd have to keep her wits about her if she were to keep him from discovering her secret.

She'd kept the awful truth from her last employer for years. She hadn't lied; she just hadn't felt the need to answer questions that had never been asked. She'd lost the position, though, regardless of her excellent job performance record, once the plant manager had found her out.

She would need to practice extreme caution when answering Joshua Kingston's questions—she planned to be truthful, as always, but that didn't mean she had to bare her soul to the man.

Tucking her purse under her arm, she started up the long, winding walkway. The air was thick with humidity as only summers in New Jersey could be. Yet, she was oblivious to the August heat as all the reasons she so crucially needed this job swam through her head; Eric needed new clothes, she owed the doctor for the last office visit when Eric had been so sick, and she still owed Mrs. Kingston for this month's rent. Next month's rent would be due in two short weeks.

Cassie heaved a sigh. If she could only convince Joshua Kingston to hire her, she needn't worry about next month's rent.

Halfway to the front door, the sound of snapping twigs caught her attention. She stopped and scanned the yard. Lifting her gaze to a movement at the side of the house, she sucked in her breath. There, perched precariously high in the tree, was a young boy. His hold on the branch looked awkward as he reached out toward a furry ball of fluff. Cassie had to squint to see the tiny kitten out on the limb.

Cassie shuddered as cold fear crawled over her skin. The boy was going to plunge to the ground, she was sure of it. Heedless of the flower bed bordering the walk, she dashed straight toward the tree.

"Here, Tinker," she heard the boy coax the kitten.

Looking up through the leaves, she could see him inching out farther. She didn't want to call out to him, afraid that if she startled him he'd lose his precarious balance.

Cassie heard the child's breath become raspy. "Oo-oo—" His voice quivered with fear. "Oh, somebody help." But he said the words very quietly.

"I'm here," Cassie called. She could see the bottom of one of his sneakers protruding over the edge of the branch.

"I think I'm in trouble, lady," he said. Then with more certainty, he added, "I'm in big trouble."

Cassie was distressed by the wheezy quality of his breathing. She could tell he was terrified. It struck her suddenly that the little boy in the tree must be Joshua Kingston's son, the child she'd be caring for. Well, this was as good a time as any to start.

"Don't look down," she told him. "Hang on, I'm coming up to get you."

She jumped, trying to grab the lowest, fattest limb of the tree, but couldn't quite reach it.

"Where can I find a ladder?" she asked.

"I need help," the boy said, this time louder.

"I'm going to help you," Cassie explained calmly, "but you need to help me, too. I can't reach the branch to climb up to you. I need a ladder. Where can I find one?"

"Um, there should be one in the . . . in the garage. Over there. Aa-aah."

Cassie heard rather than saw him slip and catch hold. Her heart leapt into her throat and the kitten mewed plaintively. Two green leaves sailed lazily toward the ground.

"Don't point," she said. "Just hang on with both hands."

"Around back," he said. "Around the house."

"Okay, listen—"

"I'm gonna fall."

The helplessness and fear he conveyed tore at Cassie's emotions. She tried to gauge just how far he was from the ground. If he did tumble from the tree, there was no doubt he'd be seriously injured.

"I won't let you fall," she promised.

When he started to cry, she knew she needed to calm him before she went off to find the ladder.

"What's your name?" she asked, using a soothing tone.

"Andrew."

"Listen to me, Andy. I want you to sit down, wrap your legs around the branch and lock your ankles together, okay?"

Without speaking, he followed her instructions.

"Now, hold on tight." She watched him clutch the limb with all his might. Her clear, unruffled directions seemed to give him a small bit of security. "Now," she continued, "I'm going to get a ladder from the garage. I'll be back in about one minute. Can you hold on that long?"

"Only one minute?" he asked.

"Yep. In fact, why don't you count slowly and I'll be back before you get to sixty."

"One . . . two . . ."

Throwing her purse at the base of the tree, Cassie raced around the house and was relieved to find the garage door open. She found the ladder hanging on the wall and lifted it off the hooks. She hurried back, lugging the aluminum stepladder.

"Thirty-seven—"

"I'm here, Andy," she called, her voice sounding a bit breathless. "And thirty-seven seconds *must* be some kind of record." She fumbled to open the ladder, talking constantly to keep the boy's mind occupied. "I'll be up there before you can say 'Sally sells seashells by the seashore.'"

After checking to make sure the ladder was secure, she kicked off her low-heeled pumps, climbed the rungs and stepped onto the lowest tree branch. "Or how about 'big brown boxes bursting with blue balloons.'"

She saw Andy open his eyes, his mouth cracking into the beginnings of a smile. She still couldn't reach him, so she hoisted herself onto the next highest limb. Her knee scraped against the rough bark and she winced.

"I know one more. 'Four fat frogs feasted on fluffy fried feathers.'"

Pulling up face-to-face with him, she returned his grin. He looked so relieved to see her. She noticed his breathing wasn't nearly as labored as it had been before.

"'Four fat frogs,'" he began, and then he relented to a wheezy chuckle.

The branch wobbled and Cassie's eyes darted toward the ground.

"No laughing, now."

Sliding her hands over his thin arms, she felt his fatigued muscles quaking and knew he couldn't hold on much longer.

"How in the world did you get up here?" she asked. "I couldn't even reach the first branch."

Before he could answer, the kitten gave another pitiful cry.

"Tinker's scared," Andy said.

"We'll get you and Tinker down as soon as we can."

"Can't go down," he informed her. "Gotta go in."

"In?" She looked at the side of the house and saw an open window. "I see."

She shook her head and laughed, despite the situation. "Actually, it would probably be easier to get you in than get you down, don't you think?"

"All I know is I want to get somewhere."

"Okay," Cassie said, calculating the length of the branch between Andy and the window. "I want you to inch backward, a little at a time."

He craned his neck to judge the distance himself. "I don't know..."

"Have you ever seen an inchworm bunch up the back part of his body?" Cassie was pleased to see that she'd gotten his attention. "Then the front part moves forward."

"Yeah."

"Well, we're going to do that, only backward. Push your body back and then wiggle your legs toward the window. Simple, right?" Cassie only hoped the suggestion worked as well in practice as it sounded in theory.

Grasping his forearms securely, she said, "Let's try."

Getting Andy back into his bedroom was surprisingly easy once she started him moving. But once inside, he was upset that Tinker was still mewing out in the tree.

"I'll get the little rascal." And Cassie inched her way along the branch to the kitten, then back again, handing the furry creature through the window.

"Oh, no," Andy wheezed, his voice filled with dread. "It's Dad." He grabbed a small aspirator, inserted the nozzle into his mouth and sucked deeply on the medication.

Cassie looked through the branches and saw a tall, dark-haired man standing at the back corner of the house. He frowned as he searched the yard with his intimidating gaze.

"Please don't tell on me," Andy pleaded in a whisper, snatching the kitten to him. "Dad will be so mad. I'm not allowed to climb the tree."

With that, Andy slid the window closed and pulled down the shade, leaving Cassie, literally, out on the limb.

She stared at the closed window a moment and then peered down through the leaves. Joshua Kingston had caught sight of the ladder under the tree and was walking toward it. How on earth could she explain? The professor's brow was deeply creased; he didn't seem at all the type of man who would appreciate a half-baked explanation of any kind.

"Please let this be a bad dream," Cassie groaned as she carefully began to make her way toward the ground.

Joshua stopped by the ladder. He didn't have time for these neighborhood kids' shenanigans at the moment. He had a plane to catch and he was already running late.

He didn't see anyone on the front lawn. Grasping a cool metal rung, he looked up into the tree. What he saw was a mile's worth of firm, feminine legs. There was no end to them. As soon as his brain analyzed the sight and alerted him to the fact that he was looking up a woman's skirt, Joshua quickly averted his eyes.

"Excuse me," he called.

"I'm sorry," the woman said as she scrambled through the branches. "I'm really sorry."

Joshua watched her descend the ladder and was powerless against the cheek muscle that insisted on tugging one corner of his mouth into an appreciative grin as he admired the pair of shapely calves that were now at his eye level. He couldn't prevent his gaze from following the runs in her stockings over her cute little knees, past her well-defined thighs, all the way up to— The soft, flowing material of her skirt *swished* to cover his view.

She hurried down the ladder and Joshua saw trim hips, a tiny waist, firm, rounded breasts, and then a long, graceful neck pass before his eyes. Then, when he was certain he would finally glimpse the face that belonged to this gorgeous body, she erroneously turned one rung short of the ground and fell hard against him.

"Whoa!" he said, clasping her to him in an effort to steady them both.

"Professor Kingston," she said in a rush, "I'm so very sorry."

Her voice was like a lively song. He couldn't wait to see the mouth that formed the sound of his name so liltingly.

The woman lifted her chin, brushing heavy, dark tresses from her face, and looked at him with the bluest eyes he'd ever seen. Long black lashes fanned out to frame her eyes beautifully. And her lips. They were pink as blushed wine, and temptingly full. Exactly as he would have guessed.

Joshua straightened his spine and blinked hard, stunned by the realization that he was admiring this woman.

Cassie stared up at the man who held her in his secure embrace, and aggravation at herself flared inside her. It was bad enough that she was going to have to explain, without betraying Andy, why she had been climbing in this man's tree, but then to clumsily plough into him was stupid and it only made the situation worse than it already was.

She stood there, pressed against the broadest, hardest chest she'd ever encountered. *Get with it, Cassie,* she told herself. *What other man's chest have you ever chanced to slam into?* She stifled a giggle and, knowing the thought wasn't *that* funny, she realized the extent of her anxiety.

"Who are you?" he asked, his gaze more than perplexed. "And exactly what is it you're doing in my tree?"

"This tree?" Cassie automatically berated herself for the foolish parroting.

His eyebrow cocked jauntily. "You've been in another tree today?"

Cassie prickled under his sarcasm. Her mouth went dry and she swallowed with difficulty. "Well," she began slowly. "There was this kitten." She swallowed again and looked up. "On a branch."

"A cat?"

When she looked at him, he was busy searching the tree for signs of the animal. She became almost mesmerized as her gaze swept over his face. He was a handsome man. No, he was more than that. His was a face that would leave a woman speechless; dark brows, prominent cheekbones, and a long, narrow nose. His russet-tinged, five-o'clock shadow enhanced his strong, tanned jawline, and he had very sexy ears. His wavy hair was a deep, deep red and looked so shiny she was sure it would feel silky if she were to reach out and run her fingers through it.

She felt the heat from his hands penetrating the thin material of her blouse. The slight pressure he was exerting on her arms caused a warm flush to radiate over her skin and an involuntary shiver coursed through her body.

His eyes are gorgeous, she thought, absolutely engrossed in her observation. Rich brown irises flecked with gold. They were the kind of eyes that stole a woman's breath. Suddenly she realized it was because those eyes were leveled on her—and only inches away—that she could study them so closely, so intimately.

"Um, no... a-ah," she stammered, trying to recall the last words of their conversation. "Not a cat. A kitten. But I think—I'm sure... he got down on his own."

His delicious gaze narrowed with a mingling of suspicion and disbelief. He frowned and she prayed for something, anything, to help her salvage the situation.

"I don't remember you telling me your name."

The dark look on his face filled her with dread. There was no way in heaven she'd get this job after such a dreadful first meeting.

"Cassie," she told him. "Your aunt Mary sent me. Mary Kingston?"

Great, Cassie, she admonished herself yet again. *I'm sure the man knows his own aunt's name.*

"*You* are Cassandra Simmons?"

His frown turned into a scowl and her stomach lurched sickeningly. Never in a million years could she turn things around now. She just knew it.

Slowly she nodded in answer to his question and found herself wilting under his scrutiny. She lowered her gaze and stared at her shoeless feet, groaning inwardly at the tiny runs in her stockings that ran over her toes and along the tops of her feet.

Well, things can't possibly get any worse, she thought. The only thing she knew to do was the same thing she'd done most of her life—make the best of a bad situation. She'd always believed that if you acted as though you had things under control, most often the people around you would think you did.

Cassie straightened her spine and lifted her face so she could look directly into Joshua Kingston's eyes. Offering him her hand in formal greeting, she garnered all the confidence she could muster and declared, "Professor Kingston, your aunt told me that you're in need of a nanny. I think I'm just the woman you're looking for."

She watched as several emotions played across Joshua Kingston's features, but he didn't say a word. She chose to take his silence as a ray of sunshine on a very foggy day. If she could just keep talking, maybe he'd forget he'd found her climbing around in his tree and she still might have a chance at this job.

"I've had plenty of experience with children," she continued. "Nearly nine years, as a matter of fact. I've been certified by the Red Cross in first aid. I'm clean, thrifty, honest and reverent." One corner of her mouth quirked upward and she lifted her hands, palms up. "What more could you ask for in a nanny?"

He looked as though he couldn't decide whether to frown or laugh. She helped him out by smiling brightly, but still he refused to commit himself one way or the other.

"Maybe we should discuss this inside," he suggested.

"First I need to put the ladder away." She snapped it closed, adding, "An enticement like this shouldn't be left out where there are children around." She lumbered off toward the garage before he could say a word.

She turned and saw him still standing there. "Would you bring my shoes?" she asked, sticking out one foot and wiggling her bare toes. "Oh, and my purse." She didn't wait for his response, she simply headed toward the garage hoping her audacity would throw him off kilter enough that he wouldn't deny her the job just yet.

After hanging the ladder on its hooks, Cassie followed Joshua through the house and into the study. She sat down in front of a massive walnut desk, took her shoes from his hands, and watched as the professor perched his hip on the desktop. He cradled his chin in the vee between his thumb and index finger and scrutinized her from head to toe.

Cassie forced herself to sit patiently, knowing she needed to give him time to churn over all the thoughts that must be running through his head. Nervous energy roiled inside her. Why he simply didn't tell her she wouldn't do for the job, she had no idea, but his silence led her to believe there was still hope.

After a deep inhalation, he finally spoke. "I want you to know..." He paused with great effect. "That the only reason I'm hiring you—"

Elation ran through her. The job was hers!

"—is because of the high recommendation Aunt Mary gave you."

Cassie found herself staring at the movements of his mouth and she was impressed with the way he said the word *aunt,* making it rhyme with *taunt.*

"I would normally delve into your background with a great deal of fervor..."

Delve. She'd read that word in books before, but she hadn't ever heard anyone actually use it.

"But I need to leave immediately, so I'm going to bypass my regular routine about these things and go directly on instinct."

"You're leaving right now?"

Joshua stood. "Is that a problem?"

"Mary told me you were desperate for a nanny—" she straightened in her seat "—but she never said how desperate."

"Yes, well, Aunt Mary can be quite...distracted at times," he said. "She offered to watch my son, but I couldn't chance her forgetting to give him his medication if he should need it."

"Well, there's really no problem," Cassie assured him. "I didn't bring my things, but—"

"Good! Because I must catch the next flight to the West Coast. I'm due to give a seminar on a paper I had published. I didn't want to go, but I was given no choice. The nanny up and quit last week and the sitter I've been using suddenly had other plans. Unfortunately, I'm not quite finished packing, so I really do need to hurry."

"That's fine," she assured him. "But I have some questions about my responsibilities."

"I understand that," he said, moving around behind the desk. "But first I want to tell you a few things about my son." He picked up a manila file and placed it in the briefcase that sat open on the desktop. "You see, Andrew is an unhealthy child. He's asthmatic and has multiple allergies. My son needs special care." He looked at her as though gauging her reaction. "I don't allow him to play with the other children in the neighborhood—rough play often triggers an attack."

Cassie remembered Andy's wheezing when he was stuck in the tree.

"I also don't want him outside for long periods of time," Joshua said. "My son is hypersensitive to airborne pollen. Also, he's allergic to eggs. And he can't tolerate animal hair of any kind, so no pets." He narrowed his gaze. "You don't have an animal, do you?"

"Oh, no," she said, but her insides knotted as she thought of the kitten she'd handed to Andy through the window.

"Good." He reached across the desk, holding out a sheet of paper. "Here's a list of everything you need to know. Doctor's address and phone number. A number where I can be reached. I've also jotted down a list of rules for you to follow concerning Andrew."

Cassie took the paper from him and looked down at the long column of Do Nots. She couldn't believe some of the restrictions. According to the list, Andy wasn't allowed to ride a bike, run or eat candy of any kind. Then she glanced at the telephone numbers of the pediatrician and an allergy specialist.

"I'd like—"

"Just a second, please," she interrupted. "Just how sick is your son?" The frown she received made her sorry she'd asked the question.

The professor ran an agitated hand through his russet hair. "Ms. Simmons, Andrew is... How should I say it? My son has a delicate constitution. He was born prematurely, and hasn't been healthy since birth." He tossed another sheaf of papers into the briefcase and shuffled through another stack on the desk. "He must be protected."

She pictured the little boy she'd helped from the tree. The Andy she'd met might have been on the thin side and maybe a little pale, but he certainly hadn't seemed as sick as this man was making him out to be. Well, looks could be deceiving.

She glanced at the bookcases that lined the room. "Do you have any information on his condition?" she asked. "I'd like to read up on it in case of an emergency."

"Feel free." He indicated the shelves of books. "I don't really believe you'll have a problem. Andrew hasn't experienced an excursus in some time, but I don't like to take chances." Joshua moved around to the front of the desk. "Why don't I call him and the two of you can get acquainted?"

He left the study and Cassie quickly scanned the book titles, looking for a dictionary. She found one and flipped through the pages, running her finger down the column until she came to the word she was looking for.

"Excursionist, excursive," she mumbled aloud. "Ah, here. Excursus. Noun, Latin, meaning digression." As she closed the book gently and placed it back on the shelf, she couldn't help but think how, if nothing else, working in this house would surely increase her vocabulary.

She could hardly believe the interview had gone so smoothly. She had been certain that sticky questions would arise—questions that, if answered fully, would have revealed the horrible truth about her. *Just be thankful things went as they did,* she told herself as she took a seat.

Hearing father and son coming down the hall, she smiled when she heard Andrew ask, "Is she nice?" And she was astonished to find herself waiting breathlessly for the professor's answer.

"She's the kind of person who rescues kittens out of trees."

Cassie hadn't time to decide whether or not the professor's statement had carried a sarcastic intonation before they entered the room.

"Ms. Simmons, this is my son, Andrew," Joshua introduced. "Andrew, this is Ms. Cassandra Simmons."

Cassie stood and threw the boy a quick, knowing wink. "I'm glad to meet you, Andy," she said, offering her hand.

"Andy?" Joshua's eyebrows shot up.

Andrew giggled.

Cassie felt her cheeks flush pink. "I shouldn't call you Andy? I didn't know—"

"I like it," Andrew exclaimed, his head bobbing up and down. He grasped her hand and pumped it as though they were sealing a pact.

Joshua looked from one to the other and then back again. "If I didn't know better, I'd say you two had already met."

Cassie and Andy shared a pseudo-innocent smile and then Cassie said, "I think we're going to get along just fine. Right, Andy?"

"Right, Ms. Simmons."

"Oh, we'll have none of that," she told him. "We'll be spending too much time together for any of this Ms. Simmons stuff. Why don't you call me Cassie?"

A horn sounded out front and Joshua exhaled sharply. He gave his watch a darting glance. "It's the airport shuttle and I haven't finished packing."

"Go, go," Cassie said, shooing him out into the hall. "Andy and I will stall the driver."

Abruptly, as though a light flicked on in her brain, she remembered Eric. "Wait, Professor Kingston," she called out.

He turned halfway up the stairs, his distraction obvious.

"I, uh, I have a brother," she said, uncertain of how to broach the subject. "I'd like to know... Is it okay...? Can he—?"

"Sure, sure," he answered hurriedly. "I don't mind if your brother visits." With that, he disappeared up the steps, taking them two at a time.

It's not exactly what I wanted to hear, she thought, *but it'll have to do until he gets back.* What in the world would he say when he found out she didn't want Eric to visit her, but to live here with her?

"Thanks for not tellin' on me." Andy's mouth cocked in an engaging half grin.

"I didn't tell your father, but don't think that means it's okay for you to disobey him," she warned. "Climbing out onto that tree branch was dangerous and I don't want you to do anything like that again."

"Aw, I won't," he promised. "It's just that Tinker—"

"And that cat has got to go."

"Aw, but—"

"You heard me. It's against the rules. Now, where is Tinker?"

Andy glanced up the steps to make sure his father couldn't hear. "Under my bed," he whispered.

"As soon as your dad leaves, we'll put Tinker out, okay?"

Andy gave a resigned nod. "He belongs to the neighbor, anyway."

There was a knock at the door and the two of them went to let the shuttle driver in.

"Someone here going to the airport?" the man asked.

"I'm ready," the professor called from the top landing. He trotted down the stairs with an overnight bag in one hand, his suit jacket in the other.

He dropped the bag and searched his pockets. "Tickets, wallet, reading glasses. I guess I'm all set."

"Briefcase?" Cassie reminded him.

"Right," he said, and rushed into the study.

The driver picked up the overnight bag and went out the door.

When Joshua reappeared, he had his briefcase in hand. "Thanks." He smiled at Cassie.

The warmth that curled in the pit of her stomach startled her so that her breath caught and held in her throat. She made a conscious effort to slowly drag oxygen into her lungs. With that smile Joshua Kingston could charm the birds from the trees. *He certainly charmed me from one,* she thought wryly.

She watched father and son hug and say their farewells.

"You be good," Joshua told Andy.

"I will."

Then Joshua's intense gaze locked onto hers. "You'll be okay?"

"Andy and I will be fine. Don't worry."

Joshua's eyes didn't waver as they bored into hers, and Cassie felt her nerves begin to jangle like a bell. Enthralled by his gaze, Cassie felt as though she were being pulled deeper and deeper—

The driver honked, breaking the spell that seemed to have captivated them both. Joshua's lips tilted into a tiny smile and he gave her an almost imperceptible nod. Again, a funny, heated feeling coiled deep in her belly. Then he turned and jogged toward the van.

As Cassie watched her new employer disappear down the road, all she could think about was Joshua Kingston's charming smile—and her peculiar reaction to it.

Chapter Two

The jet engine hummed steadily as Joshua stowed his briefcase and settled himself into the seat. He hadn't wanted to go on this trip. He'd put it off and put it off until Dean Lasher had reminded him of his original agreement with the university: that of not only teaching, conducting research and publishing the results of that research, but also of traveling to other colleges and corporations to speak on his findings.

Joshua knew very well that his seminars afforded the university a certain amount of prestige and publicity, publicity that went a long way in procuring monetary donations from the businesses he visited. So he understood and was not offended by Dean Lasher's gentle prodding.

It wasn't as though Joshua was careless when it came to his profession, not by any means. He worked hard preparing lessons for his students and made cer-

tain he was always available for the young men and
women he taught. He spent hours in the lab on his research, and even more hours writing the papers that
were successfully published in numerous scientific
journals. But he couldn't argue with the dean when the
man had pointed out that the travel had ceased. At
least it had for the past three years—ever since the
death of Joshua's wife.

Memories of Elizabeth's last days brought a cloud
of guilt that fogged his brain. *You're an intelligent
man,* a familiar, accusatory voice echoed in his head.
*You should have seen the signs long before the acci-
dent.*

Clenching his jaw, he forced the dark thoughts
aside. He must atone. He knew that. And he was trying. With Andrew.

Joshua shook his head. He still couldn't believe he
had left his son in the care of a virtual stranger.

He took a moment to remind himself that the
stranger had the highest recommendation from his
aunt, had first-aid certification and eight full years'
experience with children. The new nanny may be a
stranger, but he was certain she was a competent
stranger.

Cassandra Simmons.

He was utterly amazed by the rush of adrenaline
that shot through his body just at the mere thought of
her name. It was absolutely illogical.

Unbidden images of her filled his mind as though
she were flower-scented air that permeated every nook
and cranny of his brain. The open smile that widened
her temptingly full lips. Her perky little nose. Those
alluring cobalt eyes—eyes that held an impish gleam

as though Cassie knew a secret she intended to reveal to no one. He chuckled at the thought. God, she was cute.

After rubbing his fingers across his jaw in deep contemplation, he placed his elbow on the armrest and cupped his chin in his hands. He could feel the raw hormones coursing through his body and he frowned. Cassie Simmons conjured feelings and desires in him that he hadn't experienced in a long, *long* time.

"Fasten your seat belt, please." The flight attendant touched his shoulder and continued along the narrow aisle.

As he moved to follow instructions, Joshua's analytical mind rationalized that having unwittingly viewed Cassie's long, sexy legs, firm thighs, trim hips and lush breasts as she'd descended the ladder from the tree had to be the explanation for his reaction to her. This purely physiological response to a beautiful, well-built woman was normal. Of course it was.

Unfastening the top button of his shirt, he loosened his tie and sighed. He felt better, relieved somehow, now that he understood that the thoughts invading his mind were quite natural.

He pulled from his breast pocket the index cards on which he'd jotted notes for his seminar. But try as he might, he couldn't seem to focus. Closing his eyes, he leaned his head against the padded seat back. Immediately, Cassie's twinkling eyes gleamed at him, her sunny fragrance filled his nostrils and his blood raged. *Normal,* he told himself. *Quite normal.*

"You got the job!" Mary Kingston hugged Cassie and kissed her on the cheek. "I knew you'd win

Joshua over." She gave Cassie's shoulder a grand-motherly pat.

"Mary, the man didn't have much choice in hiring me, now, did he?" Cassie sprinkled the question with light sarcasm. "You didn't tell me he had to leave so soon. We barely had ten minutes to get acquainted before he had to run out the door."

Mary's soft wrinkled brow creased even more with a befuddled frown. "I didn't mention that he was leaving to give one of his seminars? I'm almost certain I mentioned that." The old woman shrugged. "As you get older, the mind begins to rust, you know." She smiled brightly. "But everything turned out for the best."

"It sure did," Cassie agreed, her heart constricting with the deep emotion she felt for this woman.

Mary Kingston had been a friend of Cassie's grandmother's and Cassie loved the lady dearly. Mary had been a godsend two years ago; when Cassie's mother died leaving Cassie sole guardian of Eric, Mary had contacted her with an offer of help. And help Mary did, insisting that Cassie and Eric live in an upstairs apartment in a house the woman owned across town and then going even further by setting the rent rate ridiculously low. And when Cassie found herself dealing with the crisis of unemployment, Mary had once again unselfishly and generously intervened with a recommendation to Joshua Kingston.

Cassie gazed out the window to check on Eric and Andy, the steady tap, tap of Mary's knitting needles lulling her into a hazy trance.

Crisis had seemed to be Cassie's middle name since the age of fifteen. Her father had died in a freak accident at the small processing plant, a fly-by-night company that hadn't bothered with insurance. Cassie's mother had felt somewhat avenged when the company went bankrupt. But justice had been bittersweet because the lawyers had reported that, after all was said and done, no compensation would be forthcoming for Mrs. Simmons and her teenage daughter. Cassie's mother sank into a black depression.

And barely one month later, when Cassie celebrated her sixteenth birthday—which was anything but sweet—she discovered her mother was experiencing a menopausal pregnancy. This turn of events only seemed to darken Mrs. Simmons's despair.

Losing her husband and realizing her desperate economic predicament was more than the woman could take. Then, finding herself expecting a baby in the midst of such dire circumstances, Mrs. Simmons refused to fight back and simply let the unfortunate situation snuff out her spirit.

Cassie had watched her mother descend deeper and deeper into the bleak pit of anguish and grief until the woman was no longer able to take care of herself, her daughter or the baby boy she had given birth to.

"You're dwelling on it again, aren't you?" Mary's gentle voice pulled Cassie from her bleak reverie. "You're thinking about your decision, wondering whether you did the right thing all those years ago."

Her throat tight with suppressed emotion, Cassie could only nod.

"I can't tell you if what you did was right or not. But someone had to take over," Mary remarked candidly. "You had a mother who stopped being a mother, and you had a baby brother who was going hungry."

Hearing the stark truth spoken aloud only magnified Cassie's emotional response to the memory of her past. She dragged oxygen into her lungs through strangled air passages and she fought the threatening tears by blinking several times, hard.

Mary's voice became whisper soft as she said, "You did the only thing a sixteen-year-old could do. You quit high school and found work." Then her tone took on a gruff straightforwardness meant to comfort. "You took the lemon that life gave you and you made lemonade. When one job wasn't enough, you found another. And the whole time you ran back and forth taking care of your family as best you could." Mary's eyes glittered with pride. "You have spunk, Cassie. You have the courage of three women."

Cassie sighed and forced herself to smile. "Thanks for trying to cheer me up. It's just that . . . sometimes . . . when I look at Eric, I feel so badly that he'll never know his mom and dad. All he's got is me, an uneducated, worthless—"

"Don't you ever say that again!" Mary's admonition was sharp.

Refusing to relent, Cassie said, "Well, look at me. I got fired from my last job. I'm flat broke and—"

"Now, now," Mary said, her angry tone quickly replaced by grandmotherly encouragement. "None of that was your fault. You can't be blamed just because a company needs to cut back."

"What's so infuriating is that I had more seniority than some of those other overeducated idiots." Cassie flung her hand up in agitation. "I could work rings around each and every one of them. Why, I could produce more..." Her voice trailed off and she lowered her head. "But they all had something I didn't. And the minute the truth came out, I was history."

"Now, you look here," Mary said. "There's nothing wrong with you. You've just had a run of bad luck. Stop thinking bad thoughts. All that's in the past. You've got a new job now. A job that offers Eric a lovely home to live in and plenty of good, wholesome food, and—"

"But if Professor Kingston finds out..."

"Would you just hush up about it," Mary scolded. "Joshua's not going to find out anything." Her wizened eyes crinkled as she added, "No one would ever guess you'd dropped out of high school. You're so bright. If I didn't think so, I'd never have recommended you to my nephew."

Cassie's eyes softened. "I'm sorry. I didn't mean to dredge it all up again."

"Nonsense. You needn't apologize to me, Cassie Simmons. Why, we're almost family, you and me, and little Eric out there." Mary picked up her knitting needles and pulled more yarn from the skein. "I love you both dearly and I just want to see you happy. That's why I sent you to Joshua. He'll make things right for you, and you'll be helping him out at the same time. It's a perfect arrangement."

Cassie conjured an image of Joshua Kingston as he'd stood at the door to leave. She'd been jolted to the core by his smile—a smile that had transformed his intense handsome features to drop-dead gorgeous. Cassie lifted her eyes to Mary's face as a flicker of doubt crossed her mind.

"I wouldn't say the arrangement is perfect just yet," Cassie said ruefully. "I didn't have a chance to tell the professor about Eric."

"Eric?" Mary paused for a moment. "Why, I'm almost certain I told Joshua about little Eric." Then she cocked her head a fraction. "At least, I think I mentioned Eric. No," she argued with herself, "I'm sure I mentioned him."

Cassie repressed a smile at the old woman's forgetfulness. Cassie knew Mary's heart was in the right place, and that it was made of pure twenty-four-carat gold.

"Joshua didn't seem to remember Eric," Cassie replied gently.

"It's good to know someone else's mind is rusting, besides my own." Mary chuckled, her eyes twinkling as she placed the blame of absentmindedness on Joshua.

"It looks as though I'll just have to remind him when he gets home." Cassie opened the door and called the two boys to come in. Then she turned back to her friend. "Mary, we're going to have to go so I can pick up our things from the apartment. It'll take us a while to get settled and I'd like the move to go as smoothly for Eric as possible."

"Oh, he'll do just fine," Mary said. "He's really looking forward to getting to know Andrew. And Joshua will make a wonderful father figure for him."

"I don't know about that," Cassie commented dubiously. She shook her head. "The professor seems so restrictive with Andy. I mean, I understand about the asthma, but..."

"Andrew was such a sickly baby," Mary was quick to answer. Then she pursed her lips in disgust. "And all those nannies coming and going. It's been awful for both Joshua and little Andrew."

"Speaking of all those nannies, why did they all leave, one right after the other?" Cassie asked.

"Couldn't follow the rules, I guess."

"But all those rules make it hard for Andy to—"

Cassie was interrupted when Eric came charging into the house.

"Cassie, Cassie! You should see the shot Andy just made!"

Eric's exuberance was infectious. "Andy's good at marbles, is he?"

It had been hard to find a game for the two of them to play, what with all the rules governing Andy's activity. Eric was a sports-minded boy, loving baseball, soccer, football, anything physical, and all these things were off-limits to Andy. But when Mary had mentioned marbles, even producing a small sackful, both Eric and Andy had been quick to agree.

"Yeah!" Eric clapped his new friend on the back. "Andy has a special thumb flick, and he knocked three of my marbles out of the circle with one shot."

"A special thumb flick, eh?" Cassie ruffled Andy's hair and saw the boy blush with pride over Eric's praise.

"Aw, it wasn't anything great, Cassie," Andy mumbled.

"Sure it was!" Eric turned to Andy. "You'll teach me how you do it, won't 'cha?"

A smile washed over Andy's whole face. "Sure I will."

"You boys gather up all the marbles, now," Cassie told them. "We need to be scooting home, so Eric and I can unpack."

Cassie saw that Mary had returned to the task of knitting the bright yellow square that would soon be part of a large afghan.

"Mary," she said softly, "I can't thank you enough for all that you've done for me and Eric."

"Stuff an' nonsense," the old woman scoffed. "You're perfect for the job."

"It's not just the job." Cassie knelt down by the rocker, lacing her fingers together and draping them over the arm of the chair. "It's everything. The list of things you've done for me is endless."

"And what about you chauffeuring me all over town, to the doctor, the bank. And you do all my shopping." Mary's soft, wrinkled hand covered Cassie's. "You've done just as much for me as I ever have for you, so don't feel you owe me any thank-yous."

Cassie was about to insist that Mary take the appreciation due her, but remained silent, afraid the emotion she felt would swell her throat and make her cry. "Well, just know I'll do my best to take care of Andy."

"And Joshua," Mary quickly added. "Don't forget to take care of Joshua."

Cassie promised she would, but in her heart she felt Joshua Kingston could easily take care of himself.

The rays of the Sunday afternoon sun kissed Cassie's skin as she floated on her back in the liquid warmth of the pool. She closed her eyes, letting her muscles relax, as she thought back on her busy, thoroughly enjoyable weekend.

Friday evening had been spent getting settled. Andy wanted Eric to sleep next door to him, which left Cassie with the room adjacent to the master bedroom. She didn't know why that disturbed her, but after several trips back and forth to her new room, she'd noticed that she'd become preoccupied with Professor Kingston's sleeping quarters. So much so, that she'd finally closed his door to shut off any temptation of peeking in. She couldn't fathom why she found the thought of exploring his room so enticing. Maybe she felt that by studying this most personal domain, she would gain some insight into Joshua Kingston, the man. The very idea of her thinking of the professor as a male rather than her employer had startled her so that she'd vowed to stay away from his room. Seeking out his character was not part of her job here, her business was strictly to care for the man's son.

But try as she might, Cassie couldn't completely exorcize the disturbing reflections of the intriguing man who seemed to haunt her mind. Joshua's quick, terse telephone calls inquiring as to how things were going came like clockwork and always left Cassie pondering Joshua Kingston's dark temperament. Even now she had to consciously pull herself out of this daydreamy state and force herself to concentrate on minding the boys who were paddling in the pool.

Cassie was pleased that she, Eric, and Andy were getting along so famously. They'd spent the entire weekend together with no quarreling or fussing. They'd gone shopping together because the kitchen cabinets had been bare enough to embarrass Mother Hubbard.

She was learning the kinds of foods Andy enjoyed, and which he was allowed. She felt she knew the list of restrictions by heart now. That dreaded list was her biggest problem. Finding quiet games to occupy the boys had been her toughest task all weekend. Eric suggested over and over that they play outdoors, and Andy had begged to join him. But Cassie had had to stop them from racing around more than once. She felt she'd done an adequate job so far, because she hadn't seen Andy strain to breathe or use his inhaler since she'd helped him from the tree.

When the boys suggested a swim, Cassie had consulted the list and found that the pool wasn't among Andy's restrictions. When questioned, Andy's face was angel-innocent as he swore the pool wasn't off limits. This didn't make sense to Cassie. If keeping Andy calm and unexcited had been the professor's goal, then allowing his son to swim was probably not the best idea. So she'd told the boys they could putter in the water—and puttering meant just that, no diving, racing, chasing or tossing. They hadn't liked her rule, but they'd resigned themselves to it just the same.

Rolling over, Cassie gazed across the water and frowned when she noticed how Andy clung to his inner tube.

"Andy," she called, and he stopped mid-paddle to glance her way. "Can you swim?"

His face flamed, but he looked her directly in the eye. "No," he admitted. "But it's okay since I have this." He thumped the rubber tube with his fist.

"Is that really smart thinking?" she asked archly.

"Andy wouldn't be allowed to swim, anyways," Eric commented, coming to the defense of his new friend. "His dad would rather see him drown than for him to do something as fun as swim."

"Eric!" Cassie stood up in the shallow end of the pool and stared aghast at her brother. "I can't believe you said such a horrible thing. Now, get out of the pool until you can apologize."

"Aw, Cassie."

"Now, young man."

"He's right, Cassie," Andy said, his voice soft. "Dad doesn't let me do nothing. I never knew how much I'm not allowed to do until Eric showed me."

"Dad doesn't let me do anything," she automatically corrected, but her heart constricted at Andy's sadness. "But it's because of your asthma," she explained. "You know your father's only concerned for your health."

She turned to face Eric, who was sitting on the pool's edge, his feet dangling in the water. "We talked about Andy's asthma and how he needs to stick to quiet activities." She frowned and shook her head at him. "I'm surprised at you. I'm disappointed you would hurt Andy's feelings like that."

"Gosh, Cassie, I'm sorry." Eric's head dipped dolefully. "I'm just used to playing ball and runnin' and sweatin'. And I've been playing card games and tiddledywinks for two days. I'm not used to this stuff."

Cassie sighed hard in an effort to suppress her amusement at his description of normal play. Eric was right, though, he *was* used to playing like a normal eight-year-old boy, and he *had* been playing quiet games all weekend. She looked from Eric to Andy and felt torn over how to solve the problem.

"Well," she finally said, "how about if I speak to Andy's father when he comes home and see if maybe he'll lift some of the limits?"

"Would you?" Andy asked.

"All right!" Eric shouted.

"I'm not promising anything, now."

"Wow, Cassie, if I could just have a catch with Eric, I'd be happy!" Andy's tone spoke volumes on the exciting prospect of getting a ball in one hand and a mitt on the other.

Cassie shushed him with a waggling, upraised finger. "All I can do is talk to your dad, Andy. I don't want you to get your hopes up for something that may never happen. Do you understand?"

Andy nodded somberly.

Cassie felt badly about reining in his excitement. In an effort to make up for it, she rubbed her hands together and smiled, saying, "But there's no reason I can't teach you to swim. In fact, I think it downright necessary if we're going to be spending time in the pool."

"You mean it?" Andy asked, his smile once more beaming.

"I can help him, too. Can't I, Cassie?" Eric pleaded.

"You sure can," she said. "Andy, when we're through with you, you'll be swimming like a fish."

"And," Eric piped in, "I'll show you how to dive, like this." He pushed off from poolside and *kersplashed* awkwardly. When he surfaced, embarrassment turned his face as red as the belly flop had turned his stomach. Andy laughed and Cassie promised Eric that they'd work on his diving technique.

"But first, I need to show you a few safety pointers," Cassie said. "First and foremost, whatever happens when you're in the water, remember, don't panic."

Eric puffed his chest out and said, "Never swim alone."

"Good, Eric," Cassie praised her brother. "Now, Andy, tell me what you'd do if you accidentally slipped out of your inner tube."

"Well...I..." Andy's eyes brightened and he blurted, "I wouldn't panic." Cassie chuckled at his quick thinking.

"I'd grab for the tube," he tried again. "And paddle for the side."

"What if you fell into the water and didn't have the inner tube?" Cassie asked.

Andy's eyebrows raised and his mouth worked, but no words came out. He was thoroughly stumped.

Eric sniggered and gave Andy a friendly shove. "You better hope someone's around to call the rescue squad."

Andy giggled nervously. "Well, teach me what I should do."

As serious as water safety was, Cassie didn't reprimand the boys for their silliness. This was a scary subject, and a little humor would help Andy through it.

"You needn't worry about sinking, you know," Cassie told him. "Why does your tube float?"

"It's full of air," Andy answered with a shrug.

"And if you inhale?"

Andy's eyes lit. "Then I'm full of air!"

Cassie nodded, chuckling.

"And I won't sink?"

Again she nodded.

"Show him the dead man's float!" Eric shouted.

"Yes, yes, the dead man's float," Andy chimed in. Then he grinningly added, "I don't know what it is, but it'd be great to see a dead man float."

Both boys burst into uproarious laughter.

Andy pulled himself from the water and sat, dripping, next to Eric.

"Okay, watch closely," Cassie said. "You inhale deeply, put your face in the water, and relax your entire body."

Eric leaned toward Andy. "It's important that you inhale *before* putting your face in the water," he cautioned with a chuckle.

Cassie made a production of sucking a great deal of air into her lungs, then relaxed into the water, stretching her arms wide. She remained in position for several seconds before standing and shaking her head, spraying the boys.

"See how easy it is?" she asked. "You want to try?"

Andy was quiet, looking at the water, and Cassie saw a spark of fear in his eyes. Eric noticed Andy's silence and quickly glanced at Cassie.

"Show us again, Cassie," Eric said. He nudged Andy. "My sister makes a great dead man, doesn't she?"

The corner of Andy's mouth quirked up, and Cassie's heart warmed to see how her brother was trying to stifle Andy's fear.

"Dead man's float! Dead man's float!" Eric began to chant, clapping his hands to emphasize each word. Andy quickly joined him, and Cassie laughed.

"Okay, okay, already!" she yelled over the din of their voices.

She inhaled and let her body float. Her feet lifted off the bottom of the pool. She could hear the boys' cries of encouragement, muffled by the water. Their shouts and squeals made her laugh, the air in her lungs bubbling from her mouth.

When all the air had expelled from her body, Cassie lifted her face sideways to inhale. But before she could, a great splash startled her and a weight pushed her under the water's surface. Instead of inhaling the expected air, she took in a mouthful of water and choked, instinctively pushing away from whatever had her in its clutches.

She needed oxygen. Now!

Her head flashed above the surface for an instant and, through the heavy curtain of hair plastered across her face, she quickly gulped in half a lungful of precious air before she found herself once again floundering below depths.

She opened her eyes under water and saw the sunlight glinting off a pair of shiny black dress shoes.

Instantly she knew exactly what was happening. Cassie groaned silently. Joshua Kingston had returned home.

Chapter Three

Cassie went perfectly still in his arms and a knot of panic balled in Joshua's gut. She'd blacked out.

Firming his grip on her warm, wet skin, he hauled her out of the water with all his might.

"Cassie?" Fear clawed his throat, making his voice tight and harsh. "Cassie!"

She stood, sputtering and coughing.

He staggered over to the steps with her and pulled her from the pool and onto the concrete patio.

"Andrew," he called, "bring a towel."

"Yes, sir," Andy replied.

"Are you all right?" Joshua asked Cassie.

She nodded and swiped at the hair clinging to her cheeks as she continued to cough. Joshua wrapped the large beach towel around her shoulders and noticed how his hands were shaking.

This was a hell of an end to an already nerve-racking

weekend. He'd worried about getting back into the swing of speaking before a large audience after such a long sabbatical; he'd worried about leaving his son; he'd worried about the summer graduate courses he was in the midst of teaching. But even though all these things had weighed heavily on his mind, he'd had to admit that thoughts of the new nanny he'd hired had crept into his brain more times than he could count. And images of Cassie Simmons had pushed all his worries aside. Joshua had been unable to comprehend it. His reaction to this woman—his thoughts of her—had sparked a curiosity in him, a desire to know more about her, a desire to discover why and how a woman he barely knew could stir him so deeply.

Seeing Cassie floating in the water, still as death, had frightened the devil out of him. The shouts of panic coming from the boys had only increased his alarm. Joshua hadn't thought, he'd only acted. He knew he was impulsive in emergency situations. Most often it was a trait he didn't care to have—to be unthinkingly reactionary. But in this instance, he thanked the stars for his panicky nature.

He listened intently as her choking coughs subsided. Her deep, ragged breaths were a relief to his ears. Joshua lowered his eyelids and sighed as his sanity slowly returned.

When he opened his eyes, he looked from Cassie to his son to the other boy by the pool. His gaze took in the wet towels draped over the lawn chairs and the multitude of pool toys littering the patio. More than one of the restrictions he'd given the new nanny was being broken at this very moment. The idea that Cassie Simmons had disregarded his wishes acted as a flickering match that ignited his anger.

"What the hell is going on here?" he demanded.

Cassie inhaled jaggedly and gave herself over to another fit of coughing in an effort to expel the water from her lungs.

She looked at Joshua Kingston's handsome face and the dark frown she saw there made her chest fill with apprehension. Cassie heard a tiny spurt of aerosol and glanced at Andy, who was sucking on the inhaler that had somehow magically materialized in his hand. Looking back at the professor, she saw the crease in his brow deepen to a black scowl and she wondered how in the world the pleasant day had changed so suddenly.

She coughed into her fist again and rubbed her throat with her other hand before beginning. "Believe it or not, Andy hasn't—"

"Don't bother trying to explain," Joshua Kingston interrupted harshly. "I specifically instructed you that Andrew was not to be outside. I specifically instructed you that Andrew was not to play with neighborhood children. *And* I specifically stated on the list of restrictions that Andrew was not to use the pool."

Cassie drew her shoulders back in defense. "But—"

"No buts, Ms. Simmons," he blared at her. "How could you even think about taking these children near the water when you can't swim a stroke?"

Realizing his misconstruction of the situation, Cassie stood and took a step toward him. "Professor Kings—"

"Do you realize that if I hadn't arrived when I did, you probably would have drowned?" Joshua Kingston tried to stuff his hands into the pockets of his sopping wet dress trousers. When he failed, he expelled an angry curse and slapped his palm against his thigh in obvious frustration. "Andrew could have drowned. Or him...." His angry eyes fastened on Eric. "Who are you, anyway?" Without waiting for an answer, Joshua snapped, "Go home, young man."

Eric glanced nervously at his sister and then back at the man who had shouted at him.

"Do as I say," Joshua demanded. "Get your things and go."

Pale with fright, Eric's eyes welled with tears, and Cassie's fierce motherly instinct roared inside her like a wild animal. Who was this man to think he could frighten her brother this way?

"Professor Kingston, Eric is my brother," she told him, holding tight to the anger erupting in her. "I tried to tell you about him Friday evening before you rushed off, but I didn't get the chance to explain. I'm Eric's guardian. Where I live, he lives."

Confusion passed fleetingly across Joshua's features but it was overcome finally by the deep, troubled scowl that settled in the middle of his forehead. "I see," he said, but it was evident from the tone of his voice that he didn't.

Cassie turned her attention to the boys, her calm exterior disguising the turmoil she felt at having blurted out an explanation about her brother. "It looks as though Professor Kingston and I have some things to discuss. I'd like for you two to go upstairs and change into some dry clothes and get out a quiet game.''

The boys glanced at the formidable man who stood towering a few feet from them and exchanged a look of indecision.

"It's okay," Cassie assured them. "Go on. And don't forget to hang your trunks and towels in the bathroom."

She watched the boys scurry into the house and she turned to Joshua. Those deep brown eyes of his bore into hers. Why did he have to be so good-looking? It would be easier to find the words to speak if the sight of his handsome face didn't whisk away her thoughts. She didn't know whether it was his gorgeous, chiseled features or his grim countenance that started her stomach churning again. Every time she was in his presence her nerves jangled like church bells. She clenched her fists at her sides, digging her nails into the soft flesh of her palms and hoping the pain would help her to focus.

"Professor Kingston," she said, leveling her gaze on him, "I want you to know right up front that I didn't break any rules, spoken or written."

"You didn't break any rules?" His voice was full of incredulity. "Andrew was outside. Andrew was in the pool. Andrew had a playmate." One eyebrow raised mockingly as he asked, "Did you, or did you not, see Andrew take a dose of his asthma medication just two seconds ago?"

Cassie pressed her lips tightly together. This man would never believe her if she told him Andy hadn't used his inhaler all weekend. She had no desire to be called a liar on top of everything else.

"Yes, Andy was outside," she said, determined to remain composed. "But the list of restrictions did not stipulate that he was *never* allowed outside." Her voice became tighter. "Yes, Andy was in the pool. But swimming was not restricted."

He looked as though he were about to speak, but she shot him a look that told him she wasn't finished and his jaw muscle worked in agitation as he waited. Astonishingly, Cassie found the tiny movement extremely sexy and she had to concentrate on what it was she had meant to say.

"Um, yes, Andy had a playmate," she went on. "But Eric is *not* one of the neighborhood children. He's my brother. And you *did* give your permission for him to visit."

"That *is* the operative word here," he said. "Visit. I gave my permission for your brother to *visit,* not move in." He tilted his chin abruptly and asked, "Just how old are you, anyway? Your brother looks about Andrew's age. You look awfully old to have a brother so young."

"Thank you very much, Professor Kingston," Cassie said caustically.

"No, no—" He reddened, apparently realizing how his words sounded. "I didn't mean to say you look *old,* only that you seem too old...only that your brother is..." His voice trailed off in hopeless frustration and he shook his head.

Cassie looked away. When she turned back to face him, she had the well-practiced explanation on the tip of her tongue. "I'm twenty-four years old. My mother became pregnant late in her life. She died two years ago when Eric was six, leaving me Eric's guardian."

Her chin lowered a fraction, but her eyes remained focused on his. "So, you see, Professor Kingston, if I keep this job—and I realize that it's a very big if—then Eric must stay with me."

Joshua Kingston nodded slowly. "I agree with you."

Cassie couldn't hide her surprise. "That Eric should stay with me?"

"No. That your keeping this job is a very big if."

Her spirit plummeted.

Finally he said, "I really have to question your judgment. Taking those boys into that pool when none of you can swim was dangerous, and it was stupid."

Although Cassie bristled at his choice of words, she willed herself not to respond. Her extreme sensitivity to derogatory remarks made about her intelligence was her problem, not his.

"You don't understand—" she began.

"It was more than stupid," he continued heedlessly. "It was asinine."

Cassie clamped her jaw shut and ground her teeth together to keep from spitting some horrible rejoinder at him.

Anger smoldered in her chest. She knew he had no idea of what was happening here; that she was an excellent swimmer, that Andy and Eric had been perfectly safe, that Andy hadn't needed or used his medicine in two days. But she couldn't help feeling offended by this man's presumptuous manner. She'd thought intelligent, deep-thinking men such as Professor Joshua Kingston were supposed to be open-minded, were supposed to gather all available information before making a definite decision.

Her eyes narrowed as she gathered her wits about her. It wouldn't do for her to tell the man off. He was Mary's nephew, if nothing else. She was about to lose this job, she was certain of it. So she quickly made her own decision; she'd quit before he had the chance to fire her. At least that way she could salvage some of her dignity.

"Professor Kingston, I understand that you wouldn't want to leave your son under the care of someone whose judgment you can't trust." She picked up the worn terry robe she'd brought down to the pool with her and slipped her arms into it. "I'll pack up our things, and Eric and I will be out of your way as quickly as we can." Pulling the ends of her belt, she made a tight knot. "I'll call Mary about moving back into my apartment."

Without waiting for his response, Cassie turned and walked quickly toward the house, certain that she couldn't bear another of his insults without telling him how stupid and asinine *he'd* been for jumping to conclusions about her and the situation.

Joshua stared at Cassie Simmons's back as she marched across the grass and he fought to control his emotions. It was rare for him to lose his temper, but saving Cassie from drowning had shaken him more than he'd realized. What might have happened if he hadn't been here? The answer to that question staggered his imagination.

He raked a hand through his wet hair and the thought from his mind. He sighed, tugging at his soggy trousers. This was one suit he'd never wear again, the chlorine pool water had irrevocably ruined it. He could feel the material shrinking as he stood there.

He sighed again, this time even deeper. Glancing across the lawn, he saw Cassie disappear through the beveled French doors. So, she was leaving. She was going to pack her bags and leave his life forever.

Why did that thought bother him so damned much? He didn't even know the woman other than the little Aunt Mary had told him. He'd spent barely a quarter of an hour with her on Friday afternoon. How could a woman crawl under a man's skin in fifteen minutes' time? It was absolutely ludicrous!

But Cassie Simmons had surely ruled his thoughts the whole weekend. He'd hardly been able to concentrate on his seminar. Those jewel-blue eyes of hers had preyed on his mind until he'd felt he'd been possessed. And the dreams he'd had! He hadn't experienced the like since his randy teenage years.

Joshua shivered in the sudden breeze. He needed to change into dry clothes, but for some reason his feet were like lead. And he felt as though he had a lump of the stuff in the pit of his stomach.

He knew Cassie Simmons's leaving was for the best. She never would have worked out as Andrew's nanny. What had his aunt Mary been thinking to recommend Cassie for the job? Imagine the woman bringing her brother here to live! He did have to admit, however, that he hadn't given her the chance to finish her sentence when she'd mentioned her brother on Friday.

But she had allowed Andrew access to the pool. He knew for a fact that swimming was on the list of restrictions. He'd quickly compiled a new list himself just before he'd left, after he'd remembered that the last nanny had ripped the old one into a dozen ragged pieces. Andrew wasn't supposed to be in the pool. He could have become overexerted—could have suffered an asthma attack.

No, Cassie Simmons was not the person he was looking for as a nanny for his son. He'd pay her for her work this past weekend and let her get on with her life. Why, though, did he have this sinking feeling that he was going to be missing something special by never having the chance to know her?

After squishing his way to the house, he slipped off his sodden shoes by the door and made his way to the staircase. Passing the library, he heard Cassie's voice.

"Oh, no, Mary. You didn't."

Joshua stood at the bottom of the steps and cocked his head as he blatantly eavesdropped.

"But how did you find another tenant so quickly?" Cassie asked. "It's only been two days."

So, Joshua thought, it looks as though Cassie and her brother had no place to go. He felt an odd quiver in his chest and couldn't decide if elation or sympathy was the cause.

"I most certainly do not want you to say a word to him," Cassie said.

He smiled, easily imagining his aunt offering to petition on Cassie's behalf. Aunt Mary was one lady who was always ready and willing to go to bat for the underdog.

"Please, Mary," Cassie stressed. "I want to do this my way. Don't worry about us. I'll think of something." She hesitated. "Mary," she said, "can I leave my stuff in your storage building awhile longer?" Cassie gave a relieved sigh. "Thanks so much."

When he heard Cassie saying her goodbyes, he hurried upstairs. After closing his bedroom door, he tugged off his trousers and tossed them over the brass clothes butler. Don't become involved in this woman's problems, he told himself. He peeled off the rest of his wet things, tie, shirt, socks, briefs, and quickly toweled himself dry. But as he pulled on dry socks, Joshua had to admit there was a part of him that was interested—too interested—in helping Cassie Simmons. And he could find no logical reason for his interest.

Just as he'd finished dressing, there was a soft tap on his door. "Come in," he called.

Andrew entered, his shoulders rounded, and took one step into the room. "Dad," he said, "can I talk to you?"

"Sure. Come on over here." Joshua raised one brow quizzically when he watched Andrew take only one step closer and then stop.

"Come here, son," Joshua gently coaxed. "After what happened out at the pool, it's no wonder I didn't get the chance to give you a proper hello. Come sit on my lap."

"Aw, Dad," Andrew lamented. "You know I'm too big for that."

Looking at the boy, Joshua pondered why he could do so few things right when it came to raising his own son. "I guess you're right. But at least come sit next to me." He patted a spot on the bed.

Andrew climbed up, settled himself on the bed and immediately began to gnaw on his thumb.

"You know," Joshua said, "your mother used to do that when she was nervous or upset about something."

"She did?" Andrew's eyes grew round.

Joshua nodded. "And you know something else?" he asked. "She was very proud of you."

"She was?" Now the boy's gaze filled with awe and pleasure. "I miss her."

Joshua nodded again but his son didn't see it as silent memories settled around them both. Finally, Joshua smoothed a palm over Andy's hair. "So," he said, "what's troubling you?"

"Well, I wanted to talk to you about Cassie and Eric."

Sensing the return of his son's earlier apprehension, Joshua softly replied, "I see."

"Dad, it wasn't Cassie's fault that we went swimming. She asked me if I was allowed and I told her yes. She checked the list and asked me if I was sure, and I told her I was. It was all *my* fault. *I* wanted to go in the pool. Dad, please don't make Cassie and Eric leave." Andrew spoke all the sentences as though they were one. Taking a deep breath, he continued. "Me and Eric played quiet all weekend. We played cards and marbles and checkers and pick-up sticks. Cassie stopped us every time we started runnin' around." He stopped to inhale again. "I like having Eric here. And Cassie took real good care of me. Please, Dad, please don't fire Cassie. Don't make her go away."

Seeing tears well up in Andrew's eyes, Joshua's frown deepened. Never had Andrew come to the defense of any of his previous nannies. In fact, when each of the women had quit for one reason or another, his son had actually seemed relieved.

Joshua rubbed his hand back and forth across his jaw. Cassie Simmons and this little Eric fellow had certainly come to mean something to Andrew over the past two days.

"Well, Andrew," he said gently. "I didn't discharge Cassie. But I am certain she intends to leave. She was just on the phone with Aunt Mary about renting an apartment."

"But, Dad, we gotta stop her! Eric's my friend. I don't want them to go."

The desperation in his son's voice squeezed at the very heart of him. Suddenly the most important thing in the world was to comfort Andrew, make his distress disappear.

"Look, son," Joshua said, clasping Andrew's knee. "Let me go down and talk to her."

It was as though the sun had risen, so brightly did his son's face shine. "Would you, Dad?"

For one quick moment Joshua felt doubt niggling the fringes of his mind. Was he about to do the right thing?

He was taken off guard when Andrew threw his arms around his neck and hugged him fiercely. Closing his eyes, Joshua let the love he felt for his son fill him to the brim with soul-wrenching warmth. He'd persuade Cassie Simmons to stay if it was the last thing he did. For Andrew's sake.

"I'll do my best," he said.

The two of them went out into the hall together.

"Go in and play quietly with Eric," Joshua said. "I'll talk to Cassie."

Stopping at the bedroom door adjacent to his own, Joshua could hear Cassie sliding out drawers and thumping them closed.

He knocked lightly three times and waited.

"Come on in, Eric," she called.

Joshua opened her door and leaned into the room. Her face was turned away as she bent over the bed folding clothes and stuffing them into a suitcase. She hadn't changed out of her bathing suit and terry robe, and the robe gaped open at the bottom to show a slice of creamy thigh. Joshua's pulse quickened, his heart thumped in his chest, and he was once again amazed by his reaction to the sight of this woman.

God, but she's got beautiful legs. He stared, unable to speak. Her tiny feet were perfectly shaped and Joshua pictured himself slowly massaging them as though it were the most natural thing in the world. Before the vivid image in his mind could progress further, he cleared his throat to alert Cassie to his presence.

She jerked a quarter turn to face him, her eyes wide with surprise.

"Could I speak with you?" he asked.

Curiosity flitted across her face and she nodded.

"Downstairs in the library," he suggested. "Whenever you're ready."

"I'll be down in five minutes."

He closed the door between them, took his time going down the steps and into the library. He relaxed into his chair and took several deep breaths, but his heart continued its illogical, yet nonetheless furious, racing.

* * *

Cassie had never dressed so fast in her life. After tugging out of her damp swimsuit, she slipped on a pair of panties and threw a cotton dress over her head, her fingers flying over the buttons. She ran a brush through her wet hair and braided it quickly with trembling fingers.

She didn't want another argument with Joshua Kingston, she had too many other things on her mind right now. Where she and Eric were going to stay tonight took precedence over everything.

Mary had rented the tiny apartment out to a college student who was in dire straights. Well, this particular college student's gain was certainly Cassie's loss.

She certainly regretted her quick and angry reaction to Joshua. She wished now that she hadn't quit this job.

How was she going to tell Eric that they had no place to go? she asked herself as she moved out into the hallway, closing the bedroom door behind her. At least Joshua owed her wages for the weekend, she remembered. Maybe she and Eric could stay in a cheap hotel for the night. Maybe she'd find an apartment tomorrow. Maybe she'd find a job. Maybe...

All these maybes were driving her crazy! What on earth was she going to do?

Cassie tamped down her rising panic. She could handle this. She'd handled worse, hadn't she? Right at this moment, facing Joshua Kingston for the last time was what she needed to focus on. She knew she had to remain calm, cool, and collected. She didn't want to become angry, because then she just might say something that could make him decide not to pay her at all. Her apprehension soared toward hysteria. She needed that money!

The muffled sound of Eric and Andrew's laughter made her stop short. Looking around at the welcoming walls of this house, she wondered where she'd be later on this very evening. In some cold, impersonal hotel? Or worse yet, would she and Eric end up sleeping in the car?

The questions made her skin prickle with icy fear. With no place to go and no money to get there, Cassie felt more than frightened; this whole mess left her desolate inside.

Suddenly feeling weak in the knees, she crumpled down onto the step at the top of the stairway and cradled her head in the crook of her elbow. She gulped in air to try to calm herself. She'd gotten through bad situations before, she'd get through this one.

Dark memories flitted through her mind, memories of herself—a young woman left with a six-year-old brother and no clue as to where to turn. And through sheer tenacious persistence and lots of luck, that young woman had survived. So far. But it looked as though her luck may have just run out.

Her eyes followed the heavy, solid banister that ran down the length of the wide staircase. Her gaze ran over the wallpaper-covered walls. This was a good house, a solid house, a warm house. It was a much better place for her and Eric to be than some cheap hotel.

Joshua hadn't fired her. Maybe, if she apologized, she could turn those odds around and keep this job.

But he'd called her stupid. Asinine even!

Lifting her chin, she resolved not to let her own pride get in the way of keeping this job. Especially when Joshua could provide a warm bed and a hot meal for Eric.

So what if he'd called her names? He'd only voiced them because he hadn't known all the facts. What she needed to do was go down there and calmly explain things to him.

Maybe if she apologized for the mix-up about Eric, and then explained about the swimming not being on the list of restrictions, perhaps Joshua would understand and let her remain here as Andy's nanny.

She stood and smoothed her palms down the skirt of her dress, hope bringing a tiny ray of sunshine to her heart. Why then did her feet seem as though they were nailed to the floor and her stomach churn with the dread one might feel when entering a cage that housed a hungry lion?

Chapter Four

Cassie stopped at the open archway of the library and took a moment to steel herself. She'd need every ounce of self-control she possessed if she was to succeed in swallowing her pride to keep this job.

"Come in, Cassie."

The professor's voice sounded strained to Cassie and her stomach twisted with apprehension. She squared her shoulders and entered the room, stopping in front of the big oak desk.

"Sit down," he said.

When she hesitated, he pointedly added, "Please."

She perched on the very edge of the chair and remembered that it was just two short days ago that she'd sat in this same seat while Professor Kingston decided whether or not to hire her. Lord, that felt like a lifetime ago.

"Professor—"

"Cassie—"

They spoke in unison, stopped, and both cracked a half smile. Cassie knew anxiety caused hers and was pretty certain that he was simply trying to be cordial even though he wanted to be rid of her.

She lifted her hand in a wordless invitation for him to continue with what he'd been about to say, but then she stopped mid-motion. If she let him speak his mind before she explained, she was certain to lose this job.

As she lowered her hand to her lap, she said, "Before you say anything, Professor Kingston, please let me explain something to you."

He laced his fingers together and rested his hands on the desktop. "I'd like to hear what you have to say."

The sincerity in his voice surprised Cassie.

After only the merest hesitation, he added, "And please, call me Joshua."

This time his tone was warm and liquid, and it sent a shiver racing across her skin. And the look in his eyes... Personal. Intimate, even. Lord, but he was handsome.

She couldn't keep the tiny frown from creasing her brow as she tried to figure out this man. One minute he was formidable and intimidating, the next he was calmly sincere and intimate. Which was the true Professor Joshua Kingston? she wondered.

"Cassie?"

His gentle prodding snapped at her attention and her spine straightened. She hastily assembled her thoughts, deciding that the best way to deal with this situation was to tell him the honest truth.

"Professor, I want—"

"Joshua," he prompted her.

She gave him a nervous nod, her tongue darting out to moisten her lips. "Joshua," she began again, then stopped long enough to swallow. "I want you to know right up front that . . . I need this job."

He opened his mouth to speak, but she stopped him with one upraised hand. "Before you say anything, please let me assure you that I took excellent care of Andy this weekend. I know it sounds as though I'm tooting my own horn, but . . . well . . . there's no one around to do the tooting but me. Andy and Eric got along very well. I kept them busy with quiet games. And I know you're not going to believe this, but Andy didn't use his inhaler once while you were away. I was going to tell you that when we were all out by the pool, but—"

"Ah, yes," Joshua interrupted. "The pool."

By the way he said the words, Cassie instinctively felt he was spoiling for a fight. Anxiety knotted in her belly, but she refused to back down on this. The pool was not on the list of restrictions he'd given her and she would not allow him to dispute that fact. She stood abruptly and plunked her fist onto her hip. "Now, Professor—"

"Joshua."

This time his reminder, accompanied by an uplifting of his dark eyebrows, was so gentle, so beguiling, that it diffused every bit of tension that had thickened the air between them only a moment before, and it confused her.

She must have been wrong about his being bent on arguing, she thought. For some insane reason she found herself helpless against the smile that tugged at her lips—a smile that was responding to the subtle yet abrupt change in the atmosphere.

There seemed to be an undercurrent of magnetic allure that drew her eyes to his and she wondered if he felt it, too. He returned her smile almost as in answer, and she shook her head thinking again how his good looks simply whisked away her thoughts. What had they been talking about? Oh, yes, she remembered. The pool.

Averting her gaze, she sat back down, took a deep breath and started again. "Joshua, I really feel it's necessary that I point out—"

"That the pool wasn't on the list," he said, finishing for her.

Her gaze flew to his and he nodded.

"You see, I checked the list," he said. "It's right here on my desk."

A smug expression crept across her face and then stubbornly lingered there. He chuckled.

"It's nice of you not to say 'I told you so,'" he said, his eyes lighting with a hint of sarcasm.

His easy manner made her comfortable enough to laugh at his teasing.

"I guess I was in such a hurry on Friday that I forgot to add the pool," he said.

Meaning to straighten out the other misconception he had concerning her swimming ability, she started to speak, but didn't get the chance.

"However, I must tell you that you weren't the only one to toot your horn," he informed her.

A boyish grin dallied on his lips—a grin that softened his handsome, hard-edged jawline until his features were so charming that Cassie's thoughts flew right out the nearest window. Again. She knew she'd intended on setting him straight about something, but for the life of her she couldn't remember what.

"Yes," he went on. "Andrew came into my room and told me that it was his fault about the pool. He admitted that he hadn't been entirely honest when you asked him about it. He said that he enjoyed having Eric here. That you insisted the two of them stick to quiet games. It's his opinion that you're a wonderful nanny."

The compliments spoken in Joshua's deep, rich voice sent a delicious chill up the length of her spine.

"Sounds as if Andy was quite a little musician," Cassie murmured. She couldn't help feeling a little embarrassed by the accolades, but at the same time she felt pleased knowing Andy had stood up for her.

"Mmm-hmm," Joshua said. "When my son toots, he really toots." His eyes gleamed with warmth and pride, and the corners of his mouth curled upward. His gaze became reflective as he commented, "In two short days you and Eric have really come to mean a lot to him. He's never come to the aid of even one of his nannies before this."

Cassie gave a small shrug. "I'm sure it's because of Eric. Those two have gotten along so well." She related the story of Andy's famous marble thumb flick that Eric had begged to be taught.

After a moment of absorbed silence, Joshua said, "I guess I have kept my son pretty isolated."

She maintained an astute silence concerning the all-too-true statement.

But his somber countenance quickly cleared. "So, how about it?" he asked. "Are you up to remaining here as Andrew's nanny?'' He quickly added, ''With Eric, of course.''

Bewilderment made her hesitate. This had been too easy. He hadn't made her grovel to keep her job. He hadn't been high-handed or haughty or any of the things she'd been expecting.

Finally she haltingly answered, ''I'd...I'd love to.''

''Good!'' He stood and offered her his hand across the desk.

Automatically she reached out and grasped it. He didn't shake her hand as she'd expected. He clasped his other hand overtop hers, and simply held her hand in both of his. She knew very well it was meant as a sort of goodwill gesture between employer and employee, but the heat that radiated from him made her go all warm and prickly. The feel of his skin against her was...exciting.

She realized the anxiety that had weighed heavy in her stomach when she'd first come into the room was gone. And she found the emotions that replaced it were dark and mysterious.

''Andrew will be so pleased.'' Joshua smiled as he continued to hold her hand.

How about you, Joshua? she wondered. *Are you pleased?* The thoughts came out of nowhere, shocking her to the very core. And even though the questions had been silent, she felt her face flame bright red. Why would such a thing even enter her head?

She knew very well that it was because the mood between them had changed so. His easy manner and open smile had taken her by surprise and had melted the tension she'd felt about begging to keep her job. His handsome face, his warm touch, had roused the questions, she was certain. His magnetic charm had pulled and tugged at her until she unwittingly found herself pondering his reaction to her staying on in his household.

A deep sense of self-consciousness prompted her to try to pull her hand from his grasp, but he held firm. She could feel his intense gaze on her and she reluctantly tipped up her chin to look at him. And it was as though he answered her unasked questions with the expression in his eyes—an expression that was purely positive and optimistic. And something else. Something almost... sensual.

The feeling she read in his deep mahogany gaze sent a tremor of pleasure pulsing through her entire body. His eyes, his face, his whole countenance became so intense with unspoken emotion that she couldn't bear it another moment. She tugged her hand from his and slowly lowered it to her side, and when she got her nerve up to glance his way again, his expression had become unreadable.

Lord, but she was being silly. She must have imagined the warm, enthusiastic look in his eyes. Especially since he'd been so angry and told her exactly what he thought of her judgment not half an hour ago out by the pool. Besides, how could he have given her a sign in response to an inquiry she hadn't even voiced? *Come on, Cassie,* she silently scolded. *Get real!*

Still, she *had* to know what he truly thought of her remaining here as Andy's nanny.

"Professor..." She hesitated, remembering he wanted her to use his first name, and she still felt a little shy about doing so. "Joshua, you're not just doing this for Andy, are you? I mean, I know you're doing this for Andy...but I need to know that...you trust me. I need to know that you aren't going to be worried about my ability to take care of your son."

He stood there behind his desk, glanced down toward the floor, and then directed his gaze once again at her.

"Cassie, I can honestly say that I wouldn't allow you to care for Andrew if I felt you couldn't do the job."

His blunt statement and the brusque manner in which he spoke it made her all too certain that she'd misread the provocative look on his face a moment before. This was an employer assuring an employee that she would keep the job only as long as she could do the job. But that was fine with her, it was what she was used to. She understood and could deal with this.

However, she did wonder where those soft, almost enchanted feelings she'd felt toward Joshua had come from. She couldn't dare let herself become attracted to the man. Heaven above, she *would* be stupid to set herself up for such a fall.

"There are a few things we need to discuss," he said.

He motioned for her to sit, and then he lowered himself into his chair.

"It's not that I don't ever allow Andrew into the pool," he said. "It's just that I like to be present. I like to make sure he doesn't overexert himself."

"I told the boys they could only putter around in the water," Cassie assured him.

"But you should never have gone into the pool when you couldn't swim."

"Oh, but—"

"I don't mind the three of you using the pool," he said, cutting her off. "But I must insist that you let me teach you to swim first."

"But I don't need—"

"I insist, Cassie." The hard edge on his voice matched the hard gaze in his eyes.

Her mouth snapped shut. This was the employer talking—no, ordering—the employee about what was expected.

Don't let yourself become angry, she told herself. But his demand was like a fanning breeze on the embers of her anger and, try as she might, she couldn't stop the fury from flaming brightly inside her. In an effort to douse her temper, she pressed her lips together until they were bloodless.

"We'll have a light supper," he said, his tone brooking no argument. "And then we'll settle the boys in front of the television. We'll pop a nice, wholesome movie in the VCR, one that will keep them occupied for an hour or so. We want the boys to view you as an authority figure, and if they see you in the position of student, it might undermine that goal. Besides, I wouldn't want you to be embarrassed if you didn't catch on right away."

If she didn't know how to swim, Joshua's effort to save her from humiliation would have been . . . almost charming, she thought fleetingly.

But she *could* swim. Like a fish. And now that she thought about it, the snappish manner in which he'd laid out plans for how and when he would give her swimming lessons really rankled. She could feel her shoulders stiffening as her ire churned and bubbled and threatened to erupt.

Tell him. The charged words echoed in her head. *Tell him you can swim.*

But at that moment a curious calm overtook her whole being. She wouldn't tell him. She'd show him. She'd march out to the pool after dinner, execute a perfect jackknife off the diving board and perform some of her best strokes for him. She fought the sly grin that teased her lips as she imagined his shocked expression.

"How does seven sound to you?" he asked, glancing at his wristwatch.

Although it seemed as if he was asking for her input on the time for their lesson, Cassie could tell by his firm, unwavering tone that a differing opinion wouldn't be considered even if she did have the gumption to voice one.

"Fine," she replied. The crafty smile pulled even harder at her mouth, but she won over it by nibbling on her bottom lip.

She stood. "If there's nothing else, I'll go check on the boys upstairs and then start dinner."

He simply nodded and she turned toward the doorway.

As she started up the steps, she realized she was exhausted. And it was no wonder, seeing as how there had been so many dramatic twists and turns to her conversation with the professor—with Joshua, she amended. She'd felt everything from trepidation and anxiety, hope and relief, anger and irritation, up to and including an astonishing temptation and attraction.

At the top of the stairway she paused and looked back toward the library, wondering how one man could make her jump through so many emotional hoops in one meeting.

Five full minutes before the allotted swim lesson, Cassie walked across the grass toward the pool. She tugged on the belt of her terry robe and fought the wariness that had grown like a tenacious wild weed in the pit of her stomach. As much as she hacked at it, it refused to die.

She knew she should be feeling very happy about having kept her job. She should be feeling relieved that she and Eric had enjoyed a hot meal with Andy and Joshua, that she and her brother had beds to sleep in tonight. But those feelings simply weren't in her at the moment. She'd even lost the smugness she'd felt about her plans of showing off her swimming ability to Joshua.

Now a cautious apprehension sat in her chest like a heavy brick. The feeling had slowly formed all the while she had prepared dinner, and it had solidified and hardened as the four of them had sat around the dining room table eating.

She knew very well the source of this formidable feeling: her attraction to Joshua. She remembered how handsome she found him, how easily his smile made her lose her train of thought, how that certain tone of his voice caused her go all warm and tingly inside. And these things frightened her.

During dinner she'd felt his dark, contemplative gaze on her. She was certain he'd stared because he was having doubts about keeping her on to care for his son. But she began to imagine how easily those intense, dark eyes of his could make her stomach turn to jittery butterflies, how those fingers that grasped the crystal glass so gingerly might caress the skin of her hand...or shoulder...or thigh. These ideas were crazy, she knew, but she couldn't stop them from bombarding her brain.

Finally she'd had to be honest and admit that the strong feeling she was experiencing toward him was attraction—an attraction that could very well lose her this job.

Untying the belt of her robe, she let it slip down her arms, then tossed it on the nearest patio chair. She was wearing the same bathing suit she'd worn earlier this afternoon. She hoped Joshua didn't comment about it; this suit was the only one she owned. Making ends meet had been a hard task on her previous salary. Extravagances such as an extra bathing suit were all but unheard of.

She slid her fingers across her rib cage in an effort to ease the disquiet thudding there. It didn't matter what his reaction was to her swimming attire, or to her, for that matter. She had to be vigilant over *her own* reaction to *him*.

Any interest in him must be stopped at the very start. Any nuance of attraction must be squashed dead.

For one thing, Joshua was her employer. She couldn't jeopardize this job because of some silly allure she felt from him. For another, she didn't want to be hurt.

Joshua was a cultured and learned man. He'd never find a bit of enticement in the likes of her—a high school dropout. She was certain he'd find the very idea of her uneducated state contemptible.

Her head dipped in habitual self-recrimination and she swallowed nervously. She never wanted Professor Joshua Kingston to know the truth. Never.

"So, are you ready?"

"Oh." Cassie jumped at the sound of Joshua's voice, unable to stop the exclamation.

"I didn't mean to startle you," he said. "You must have been in deep thought."

"You could say that." She gave a slight shrug, hoping he wouldn't guess that she'd been thinking about him.

There was a moment of tense, staring silence. Then he tossed his towel across the foot of the white chaise longue.

"Are the boys all set?" he asked.

She was relieved when he didn't press her to elaborate on the subject of her thoughts.

"Yes," she told him. "They're watching *The Adventures of Robin Hood*. Eric's pretty excited. He's never seen it."

"Eric's never seen Robin Hood?" His eyebrows inched high.

Cassie stood utterly still as she searched his face. Had there been an inflection of critical recrimination in his question? She couldn't decide. Did he think her a horrible person because her brother hadn't been exposed to the classic movie?

Drawing herself straight and tipping up her chin, she informed him, "I borrowed the book from the library and we read it together."

She knew very well that there *was* censorious reprisal in *her* tone. She thought it rude of him to criticize how she chose to raise her brother, and she wanted him to know it.

"I wasn't finding fault." He stepped closer. "I think it's great that you monitor Eric's television time."

Looking into his apologetic gaze, Cassie felt a deep sense of self-deprecation wash over her. Joshua hadn't attacked her "parenting" of Eric. But she had attacked him, and for that she felt he deserved some kind of explanation.

"It's not that I monitor what Eric watches on TV," she said. "You see, my mother had no life insurance. When she died, I had just started a new job and wasn't making enough in salary to bury her decently. So I did the only thing left to me—I sold off some household items."

She gazed off toward the horizon, embarrassed by what she was revealing about herself.

"My mother inherited some nice silver serving pieces, some china and a beautiful antique cherry writing desk. But I still needed more money." She gave a self-conscious chuckle. "It came down to selling the color television or the washing machine." His dark, unblinking eyes drew her gaze as she finished her simple matter-of-fact rationalization with, "I needed the washing machine."

Long, awkward seconds ticked by—seconds during which Cassie had to fight the urge to run and hide. She hated the thought of his knowing just how poor she'd been. And he evidently noticed her discomfort because he took another step closer and reached out to touch her shoulder.

"Cassie," he said, his voice low and murmurous. "It sounds as though you tried to do the right thing—for your mother and your brother. You have no reason to give an explanation, or an apology. I wasn't asking for either."

His outstretched fingers exerted a gentle pressure on her shoulder that she was certain was meant to reassure. But his skin was warm and silky against hers, and his touch brought back vivid images of her nearly naughty thoughts at the dinner table—thoughts that were once again coming back to haunt her. She concentrated hard on pushing them from her mind.

"I know you weren't," she said. "It's just that I snapped at you and I felt you deserved to know why." She felt her face color and she shrugged to try to cover it. "I'm a little thin-skinned concerning my responsibility to Eric."

His hand slid down her arm until it cradled her elbow. Her heart thumped against her chest so hard she was afraid he would actually see it. She was jolted when her body physically reacted to his touch and hormones or prickly stars or something ricocheted through her system at lightning speed. Although she refused to allow herself to look down, she knew her breasts pressed distinctly and conspicuously against the thin fabric of her murrey-colored tank suit. But, thank heaven, he chose that moment to let his hand drop to his side and he turned toward the pool.

"Well, I realize I haven't spent much time with Eric," Joshua said over his shoulder. "But he acted the young gentleman at dinner. He has very good manners. You've done a good job, Cassie."

She couldn't stop her flush of pride. "Thank you," she murmured.

He bent over, placed his hand on the edge of the pool and, with one quick, neat hop, stood in the clear, waist-deep water. Turning to face her, he smiled and said, "So, should we get started?"

Lord, but it was amazing how that slight contraction of his cheek muscles could transform his stern, handsome features to gorgeously sensual. Helplessly, her gaze hesitated on his sexy lips, and then upward along his strong jawline. His dark brown eyes now held an open approachability that drew her a step closer to him.

However, she nearly shuddered with embarrassment when he obviously mistook her silence as confusion concerning his question, and gently stated, "The swimming lesson, Cassie." He grinned widely, almost knowingly. "You didn't forget, did you?" he teased.

"Oh, yes," she said, her voice a hoarse whisper. "The swimming lesson."

Let him think she'd lost track of the topic at hand. That was okay with her. She preferred looking a little scatterbrained to the idea of him realizing that she'd once again been distracted by his good looks.

"Right," she repeated louder, moving to the pool's edge. "The swimming lesson."

Chapter Five

Cassie looked down at Joshua and swallowed nervously. This afternoon when she'd first thought of the idea to flaunt her swimming abilities, she'd enjoyed the prospect of making him look the fool. She'd actually thought he deserved it. But now, after having groundlessly snapped at him and hearing his supportive response to her explanation, she felt that their relationship had somehow transcended to a higher plain. Maybe it was silly of her, but she didn't want to do anything that might damage this new and delicate understanding.

Granted, he intimidated her. And she had to admit she was a little afraid of him—well, not afraid exactly. But she *was* fearful of his finding out her secret. However, they had actually exchanged a few words of civil conversation. She'd even sensed more than a modicum of respect in the words he'd directed at her. To jeopardize that by humiliating him would not be a good idea at this point.

"Cassie?"

She blinked at him. "Uh, Joshua, there's something I need to show you."

Curiosity etched tiny indentations on his brow, but he remained silent as she walked to the other side of the pool.

The textured diving board felt rough under her feet when she stepped onto it. After walking the length of the board, she curled her toes over the end, bounced once, twice, bent her knees and lunged high into the air. It was a simple dive, but it was near perfect—her body entering the water with hardly a splash.

When she surfaced, she used a strong overhand stroke to swim the length of the pool. Nearing the far wall of the shallow end, she stopped, submerged herself and surfaced with her face tipped upward so her hair slicked back out of her eyes.

She wiped at the rivulets of water running down her face and gazed toward him for his reaction, her nerves taut as guitar strings.

When he didn't speak right away, she explained, "When I told you that I was Red Cross certified in first aid, I should have gone on to tell you that they also certified me in swimming and water safety. In fact, I had a part-time job as a lifeguard for two summers right after I—" She stopped suddenly and blanched. She'd almost said, *Right after I quit high school.* Lord, but she'd caught herself just in time. She'd never made that mistake before. Never. Joshua Kingston somehow had her feeling awfully loose-lipped. She continued, "Right after I turned sixteen."

He stared at her a moment before quietly asking, "Why didn't you tell me?"

"I tried to. But you kept cutting me off." She shrugged one shoulder and screwed up her face. "You were really angry with me when you arrived home."

"But you were lying face-down in the water," he said, his tone conveying his continuing confusion. "You looked unconscious... in trouble...."

"No," she admitted with a tiny shake of her head. "I was showing Andy the dead man's float."

"Dead man," he repeated slowly, contemplatively. "That's what the boys were yelling."

Cassie nodded, and she felt her stomach tighten as she waited to see if he would be angry. She could tell from the look on his face that he was going over the scene in his head.

"Dead man, dead man," he repeated softly, almost to himself. Then Joshua looked at her and a tiny chuckle escaped from deep in his throat. "I didn't take time to think about it. I only saw you there in the pool." Now he laughed heartily.

Relief washed over her at the wonderful, sexy sound. She tried not to, but she found herself chuckling right along with him.

"I can't believe this," he said. "I ruined a perfectly good suit. Not to mention my shoes."

She grimaced. "I know."

He laughed again. "So, you can swim."

She nodded.

"And there's no need for a lesson," he said.

She shook her head apologetically.

He heaved a sigh and it was clearly obvious he was helpless against the grin that continued to tug and tease the corners of his mouth.

Finally he turned his gaze full on her, his eyes flitting over her face—from eyes, to forehead, to cheeks, to lips, to chin, then back to her eyes.

"Oh, Cassie," he said, his voice hardly a whisper. "We need to work on communicating, you and I."

All she was able to do was nod slowly in agreement.

He looked off toward the horizon in contemplation and then chuckled softly again, this time almost to himself. Then he turned to her. "There's still plenty of light left," he said. "Would you like to take a swim?"

She smiled, and with nary a hesitation, said, "I'd like that."

They swam several leisurely laps back and forth across the length of the pool. Midway through the fourth, Cassie easily glided into a one-hundred-eighty-degree roll and began a graceful backstroke.

Swimming on her back afforded her the opportunity to watch Joshua in the water. He had good form. Strong arms. Wide, powerful shoulders. The clear, cool water sluiced over his muscled back as he effortlessly ploughed across the pool. Nearly four laps and he didn't seem the least bit winded. She was impressed.

He touched the wall of the pool and stopped long enough to say, "Race you up and back."

"You're on!"

But before the words were even out of her mouth, she saw him swimming hell-bent for leather. Gulping in a lungful of air, Cassie pushed off from the wall with all her might. She skimmed underwater as far as she could before she surfaced and began pumping her arms. Her stroke felt good, strong, efficient. And she wasn't surprised when she gained on him, then caught up to him.

She could hear his full inhalation when he turned his head and lifted his face from the water. A tremor of excitement coursed through her and she kicked her legs even harder. Inching past him, she reached the far wall scant seconds before he did. She curled into a ball, rolled over under water and pushed off for the return trip.

Cassie felt good, cutting through the water. She knew victory was just a quarter lap away.

But when she lifted her head to inhale, she felt his fingers encircle her ankle. "Hey!" she complained.

His mighty tug didn't bring her to a complete stop, but it slowed her to a crawl. Joshua continued past her.

"I won!" he shouted, jubilation evident in his tone.

In an effort to be a good sport, she finished the race. But as soon as she could, she gazed at him and calmly informed him, "You cheated."

"*I* cheated? What about you pushing off the wall?"

Her chin tipped up defiantly. "You didn't stipulate that pushing off the wall was against the rules. Besides," she added with a murmur, "the underdog must take every advantage."

Immediately she realized her mistake.

All her life she'd seen herself as just that: the underdog. With no education to speak of, she'd had to use creative thinking to seek out new and better ways of getting the job done. She invariably felt inferior to the co-workers around her, but that didn't mean she couldn't do just as good or a better job than they. Her pride had always depended on it.

But now that she'd made the hasty statement, she hoped Joshua didn't ask her to elaborate on its meaning.

"That is true," he agreed with a great deal of pomp. "And you are the underdog. Seeing as how my biceps and back muscles are double the size of yours. I did take unfair advantage."

His comment would have raised her ire had she not seen the devilish gleam in his eye.

"Are you insinuating that just because you're a man, you're naturally the better, faster swimmer?" she asked. Then she observed in a pseudo haughty tone, "If you hadn't cheated, I would have beat you easily."

His chuckle was deep and rumbly and it had a teasing quality to it. "I know," he said. "Why do you think I had to resort to blatant cheating?"

One of her cheeks ticked with a hint of a grin, and then she just stopped fighting it and laughed outright.

"You're a rotten scoundrel, you know that?" she asked.

"Mmm-hmm." His eyes glinted wickedly.

Both of them stood in chest-deep water, balancing on the narrow ledge that circumvented the deep end of the pool. Cassie stretched out her foot and traced her toe as far as she could reach down the slope that led to the very bottom of the eight-foot depth. She clung to the side for support as she fought to control her wildly thumping heart. The man was too handsome for words!

He waded closer and she felt the distinct urge to back up, but she held her ground.

"Cassie, Cassie, Cassie," he whispered, and he reached out with a fingertip to capture a droplet of water clinging to her cheek.

His touch was electric, and a pleasant bewilderment saturated her as she tried to figure out this new and extremely intimate change in his mood.

She found Joshua Kingston intellectually intimidating and sometimes a little frightening. But he also intrigued her. He had her feeling so many different emotions, he constantly kept her just a little off kilter. It was scary, yet at the same time exhilarating.

Now, as the warm tips of his fingers lingered on her cheek, a delicious warmth curled low in her abdomen. The feel of his skin on hers was as velvety as the sun-warmed water that lapped at her breasts, that swelled slowly up and down her forearms.

"You have dominated my thoughts ever since you've come into my home."

His quiet words were so astonishing that Cassie spoke without thought. "I have?" she asked.

"Mmm-hmm," he murmured.

He moved so close she could feel his warm breath brush across her skin.

"Joshua," she said, her voice very faint. "I don't think this is a good idea."

He gave her a gentle smile. "And why not?"

Cassie knew there was more than one answer to his question, but for the life of her she couldn't think of any of them. Her mind went completely blank.

"It just isn't," she said, her innate protective instinct refusing to allow her to totally surrender to the sensual mood encompassing them—no matter how much she might want to.

He'd been on her mind, too, she had to admit. Hadn't she felt the urge to take a tiny tour of his bedroom suite? Hadn't she had to literally shut out temptation by closing the door of his room? Yes, he'd been crowding her thoughts, too.

He traced a finger along her cheekbone and then his delicate touch tickled the outer rim of her ear. Instinctively she closed her eyes as a shiver of delight shimmied along her spine.

"I can't explain it," he said silkily. "But I am so attracted to you. I know what I'm feeling isn't logical, but I simply can't help myself." He gently caught her earlobe between his index finger and thumb. "I've never wanted a woman the way I want you. Never."

Something about his confession didn't seem right, but enveloped as she was in this luscious haze of sensuality he conjured, she couldn't quite come up with a reason why.

"At first," he continued, "I thought what I was feeling was purely physical. That age-old, man-woman sex appeal. I was quite certain that if I could only get the chance to kiss you senseless, then I'd exorcize you from my system."

Bending his head toward hers, he planted the barest of kisses on the corner of her mouth. A liquid heat filled her—languidly, tinglingly.

"But as the weekend progressed," he said huskily, "I realized that my thoughts of you were based on more than just the physical."

She wanted to speak, but then he kissed her again, his lips scarcely touching the opposite corner of her mouth. The question she'd wanted to ask was gone—split into a dozen broken fragments in her passion-fogged brain.

He ran his fingers along her jaw and tipped up her chin so he could gaze into her face. His dark eyes were heavy-lidded now, and Cassie felt mesmerized by them *and* the intimate aura he conjured.

"Would you mind if I conducted a little experiment?" he murmured.

"An experiment?" Her voice seemed thin and far off.

"Mmm-hmm. You see, I came up with a hypothesis." One cheek muscle twitched with an appealing smile. "The one I told you about just now, that kissing you would expel you from my mind." He chuckled, a throaty, sexy sound. "I don't believe it will work," he admitted huskily, "but I *am* a scientist. And proving and disproving theories is my life."

She closed her eyes when his palm cupped her jaw.

"So, what do you say?" he whispered. "May I kiss you?"

She answered him with an almost imperceptible nod of her head. Then she softly added, "Please."

His lips pressed to hers, velvety warm and moist. The firm, gentle pressure of his mouth sent currents jolting through her. She felt his tongue play lightly across her lips, not intruding or demanding, but testing, tasting.

Her muscles seemed to melt yet tense at the same time and she relaxed against his hard chest. His soft, springy hair brushed against the flesh that was bared by her bathing suit. It tickled in a way she found delightful.

When his arms encircled her, she felt his palms slide across her wet, bare back. She wanted to sigh contentedly but her breathlessness made that impossible—the electric charge shooting through her did, too. Once again Joshua was causing her emotions to conflict and war inside her.

He smelled of chlorine and the dark, musky aroma that was his cologne. She relaxed enough to inhale deeply and she reveled in his scent.

His lips and tongue became more ardent and she realized that he wanted more. She gladly parted her lips and her tongue met his in a slow, sensual dance of welcome.

Far in the back of her brain, she heard tiny whispers of objection echoing, echoing for her attention. But she shut them out; she ignored them. She wanted this kiss, this closeness, like she'd never wanted anything before.

But this man is your employer! This time the voice was louder, most insistent, forcing its way to the forefront of her brain.

She pulled back, ending the kiss abruptly. Staring at him wide-eyed, she made a halfhearted attempt to pull herself from his embrace.

"Joshua," she protested.

"I knew it," he said in a hoarse whisper, his gaze heavy and filled with desire. "My analysis of the data disproves the hypothesis."

"It does?" Cassie couldn't keep the question from slipping past her lips. The look in his eyes made her heart begin to race.

"Mmm-hmm. I've kissed you, yet you're still up here." He tapped his temple. "My thoughts are burning for you." Then he added wryly, "As are other various parts of me."

His insinuation shocked her and caused her sanity to return. "Joshua," she repeated, keeping her tone as level as possible. "I really think—"

He cut off her words by pressing two fingers against her lips. "Before you speak," he said, "let me examine the data and form a conclusion. My thoughts of you this weekend had me feeling like a teenager. I wanted you and thought that a kiss would be sufficient. But now that I've completed the experiment, I'm left wanting more. Much more."

She watched him rub at his chin and look off over her shoulder as he summed up their kiss. The romantic haze she'd been engulfed in cleared all of a sudden. She'd thought this "experiment" of his was quite intimate, but now she was left feeling like a lifeless utensil—a beaker or a petri dish. And she didn't like it at all.

"Hey," she called to him. And when she had his attention, she continued testily. "When you equated our kiss to an experiment, I thought you were being...romantic. But now I can see that you were serious, and I don't mind telling you that this isn't right. I'm not some laboratory specimen to be—"

"Oh, Cassie," he interrupted. "I'm sorry I offended you."

The honest contrition exposed on his face and in his voice helped her to relax a little, but the insult she felt was evident in the firm line of her lips.

"I wanted to kiss you," he said, "and disprove my hypothesis because I *knew* it was wrong. I knew what I felt for you was more than just physical."

His last few words made her eyes go wide.

"I knew," he went on, seeming not to notice her reaction, "because, I could see you were beautiful..."

He called you beautiful. The realization sank in immediately. The thought alone would have sent her heart reeling, but he'd actually said the words. Right to her face.

"And I felt this tremendous urge to kiss you," he continued. "And touch your skin...and smell your hair.... But I also wanted other things."

He hesitated, and Cassie thought she'd die in the silence of the few seconds before he explained what he meant by "other things."

"I wanted to know things," he finally clarified. "Where you were born. Your favorite food. What your hobbies are."

A delightful, numbing haze slowly fogged her brain. *But this man is your employer!* This time the silent voice of dissent was as loud as a blaring horn. She needed to put some space between herself and Joshua. She needed time to think. Precious time.

"Joshua, wait just a minute." She moved backward a foot. "Now, I will admit that there's some kind of...spark or something between us," she said. "But common sense will tell you that it's nothing more than physical attraction—an attraction that we really, *really* need to deny—"

"Oh, no," he said, emphatically shaking his head. "Haven't you heard what I've been saying? If it was a simple case of physical attraction alone, I wouldn't feel this desire to know your favorite color, your favorite season. Or your shoe size, or what you like to read, or where you went to college, or if you like to walk in the woods or...or...how you met my aunt Mary."

Her blood froze solid when he mentioned the word college. Dear Lord, if this kept up, he'd find out the truth!

"Look," she said, trying desperately to remain calm. "I work for you. You pay me money to care for your son. You weren't even certain that you wanted me for the position. It is not—I repeat, *not*—a good idea for us to become involved in any kind of relationship except that between an employer and an employee."

He scowled. "But you can't stand there and deny the fact that we—"

"That's exactly what I intend to do!" Cassie turned and swam away from him toward the ladder.

"But, Cassie," he called.

When she reached the ladder, she turned back to face him. "I don't mean to hurt your feelings. But I need this job."

With that she climbed from the pool, snatched up her robe from where she'd tossed it on the chair and headed for the house on shaky legs.

Joshua watched Cassie stalk across the lawn and he scowled. She might deny what was between them—

The thought stopped short and he rubbed his fingers over his damp chin. She hadn't denied her feelings. In fact, she'd *admitted* what she felt—the physical attraction. He couldn't help but grin, thinking that Cassie found him attractive. The very memory of her saying so was a sensuous stroke to his ego.

No, she hadn't denied what was between them—she had *renounced* it. And he wanted so badly to explore the charisma...or allure...or whatever it was that so strongly drew them together!

But Cassie obviously felt that because she worked for him, they couldn't become personally involved. He did have to admit that it was an extremely logical thought on her part. A more personal relationship between them did have the potential of raising some problems for everyone concerned. He knew that, yet his brain continued to refuse to acknowledge it. Swiping his hand in a large arc under the cool, silky water, he couldn't quite figure out why his thinking process where Cassie was concerned continued to be confused and illogical.

He pushed the thought aside and directed his attention to more important matters—investigating the potent feelings he was experiencing.

As a scientist, he prided himself on being a linear-thinking man who devoted his life to identifying and solving mysteries with the use of scientific equations and systematic experiments. If given the time, he was confident he could figure out just how to categorize these emotions he was feeling.

Joshua paddled slowly, contemplatively, toward shallower water and realized there was another factor to be considered in this parodox—Cassie's emotions. She'd admitted feeling something for him; a "spark" of physical attraction she'd called it.

His foot grazed the pool bottom and he stood. Shielding his eyes from the glare of the setting sun, he remembered the flash of fear in Cassie's gaze just before she'd made her escape. She'd tried to mask her panic, but he'd read it nonetheless.

What had caused her anxiety? he wondered as he slogged toward poolside. Was it really the fact that she thought she might jeopardize her position as Andrew's nanny? Or was it something else? Something that had nothing to do with keeping her job? Could it be memories of a bad experience from her past? Had she been hurt by someone and was afraid of falling into the same painful trap? Could it be that she simply didn't trust men, or was there some other reason?

As he pulled himself from the pool with one powerful lunge, his mind echoed with one final question. Did he truly believe he could live in the same house with Cassie and not succumb to the challenge of finding some answers?

Chapter Six

The latch clicked softly as Cassie closed the back door behind her and walked out into the still, muggy night. Slipping off her shoes, she felt the cool grass tickle between her toes and she sighed contentedly.

This was her quiet time. Both boys were tucked into bed and Joshua was still at the university. Two nights a week he taught a late class and didn't arrive home until nearly ten. Cassie took advantage of these evenings to enjoy the night air and some precious time alone.

As she passed the pool she saw the moonlight glinting on the water like a thousand dazzling diamonds. She couldn't go near this area of the yard without thinking about the kiss she and Joshua had shared nearly two weeks ago—"the experiment" as she'd come to think of it. She didn't stop at the pool, but continued meandering toward the back of the yard.

That kiss had swept her away, had fogged her thinking. She had totally surrendered to Joshua's charms before she'd even had time to realize it. Thank heaven, her subconscious had shouted the dangers at her until her attention had been captured. Thank heaven, she'd had the sense to listen!

She needed to keep this job. Eric needed for her to keep this job. She couldn't take any chances at all of Joshua discovering her secret. Because if he did, he'd fire her on the spot. Physical attraction or no physical attraction. Of that, she was certain.

So for the past ten days since the kissing episode at the pool, Cassie had tried hard to keep herself out of Joshua's way. She played board games with Andy and Eric, or occupied them with various crafts, or took them on trips to the mall when Joshua was at home. She even had them going to bed a little earlier so she could read them Mark Twain's *The Adventures of Huckleberry Finn*. Avoiding Joshua was exhausting. The worst times for her were during meals, she realized as she relaxed onto the wrought-iron seat under the oak tree in the backyard. She couldn't escape him then.

The four of them ate breakfast and dinner together. And at every meal she could feel Joshua's intense gaze on her, and she had to fight the urge to stare back. She knew very well that he had things he wanted to say to her, she could read it on his face. Thankfully, he never talked about anything personal in front of the children. However, just the feel of his dark eyes on her was enough to keep her as tense as a tightly coiled spring.

Gazing up through the tree branches at the fat full moon, she tried to focus on the sound of the chirring crickets. However, thoughts of Joshua hovered near, destroying any chance of tranquillity for her on this beautiful summer night. But this was nothing new. In fact, she'd become accustomed to the way he would intrude on her thoughts no matter the time of day or night.

Some of the statements he'd made all those days ago at the pool continued to haunt her—something about what he'd said wasn't right. If the situation were different, she might have been able to ask him some questions. She wished she could talk to him and quell her confusion.

Joshua, she imagined herself saying, *what did you mean when you said—*

"Cassie?"

She gasped, and swinging her gaze up and around, she found herself looking into Joshua's inquiring gaze.

"J-Joshua..." She stumbled over his name, feeling flustered and unprepared. Glancing at her wristwatch, then up at him, she continued in a rush. "I meant to be in before you got—" She choked off the rest of the sentence. "I mean..."

He lifted his hand. "It's okay," he said, his tone gentle and understanding. "I know you've been hiding from me. That's why I made it home a little early tonight. I wanted to catch you before you went up to your room and shut me out."

The fact that he knew she'd been avoiding him made her flush with heated embarrassment and she was grateful for the shadows cast by the old oak tree.

"I want to talk to you," he said. "May I?"

He indicated the space on the seat next to her and she understood he wanted to sit down.

She nodded her assent, it was the only mannerly thing to do, and when he joined her, she immediately noticed just how small the wrought-iron seat was. He rested one ankle on the knee of his other leg.

They sat in silence, and as the seconds ticked by, Cassie's stomach knotted tighter and tighter.

"It's a beautiful night. The moon is so... luminous."

His voice had that husky quality that she remembered so well as the one he'd used during "the experiment." The tone that had had her melting in his arms. Alarm bells clanged in her head.

"What did you want to talk to me about?" she asked stiffly.

"Cassie." He chuckled throatily. "I love the sound of your name on my lips."

"Joshua, please."

"Why won't you—"

"Joshua." The crispness of her voice thoroughly severed his question. She twisted to face him. "I am Andy's nanny. Did you need to talk to me about your son?"

"Well, that's one of the subjects I'd like to discuss."

"Fine," she said. "What is it you'd like to know?"

He, too, turned in the small seat. His knee brushed her thigh and he placed both feet on the ground to give her more room.

"You've been here nearly two weeks," he began. "How are things going? With Andrew and Eric, I mean."

"Those boys act like they've known each other forever," she said. "They get along so well it's scary."

"That's good."

There was a moment of silence and the tension once again hummed like a live wire.

He studied her for several long seconds before asking, "And how are you liking the job?"

She couldn't help but smile. "I love it," she answered quietly. "Andy's a wonderful little boy. He's very..." She hesitated, searching for a word. "Studious. He reads lots of books and has a lot of different hobbies. Eric just loves looking at his coin collection."

While she talked, he lifted his arm and rested his elbow on the seat back, which left his hand dangling a fraction of an inch from her arm. She could feel the heat of his body. The intoxicating aroma of his cologne wafted toward her and she fought the impulse to pull great quantities of it into her lungs. The magnetism she felt was strong, nearly a tangible thing. Lord, but it frightened her.

"I've been so busy," he told her. "I feel as though I haven't spent much time with my son lately."

"And you should," she said without hesitation. "Andy loves you very much. He looks up to you. He's always telling Eric and me stories of how you did this or that. Andy is very proud of you."

Joshua's smile stole away her breath.

"You'll never know how nice it is to hear that," he replied.

Bolstering herself with a deep breath, she said, "He's been after me to talk to you."

"Oh?"

"Yes." She nodded. "About the list."

"Now, Cassie—"

"He wants to have a catch with Eric," she rushed on before he refused to listen altogether. "He's been begging for a real leather mitt. Throwing a baseball wouldn't exert him too much. And he's hardly used his medicine at all. I can't see why..."

"Wait, wait." Joshua only had to lift his fingers a fraction to touch her forearm in an effort to quiet her. "Just slow down a minute."

A pulsing heat emanated from the spot where his fingers gently pressed against her arm. She knew she should pull away, but at the same time she also recognized the strong desire to do just the opposite. She would have liked nothing more than to lean toward him—to feel his touch on more than just that one tiny area of her skin.

She glanced down at his hand on her arm and then up into his eyes. As she searched his gaze, her emotions waged a horrific battle inside her. She was almost becoming used to this topsy-turvy state in which she always found herself when she was in close proximity to Joshua.

"You're right," he said softly. "Andrew should have one."

"One what?" she asked, realizing instantly how preoccupied the question sounded. "Oh, yes," she quickly amended. "A mitt."

Damn, why did he always seem to muddle her thinking to the point that she looked an idiot?

"I'll have some free time this weekend," he said. "We'll go to the sporting goods store at the mall and pick one up."

"Andy will be happy to spend some time alone with you."

"Oh, but I meant all of us," Joshua said. "Eric will need a new mitt, too."

Cassie thought of the worn and tattered glove that she'd purchased for her brother at the secondhand store. Then she lowered her gaze.

"But his mitt is okay," she said awkwardly. The glove really wasn't, but she didn't have the funds for an expensive new one.

"But I want to buy him a new one," Joshua insisted.

"Oh, but I couldn't let you—"

"No arguments."

His hand closed on her arm and her throat convulsed in a swallow. They fell silent again, and although she forced herself not to look, all her attention focused on the velvet heat where his skin contacted hers.

He slid his fingers upward until his palm rested on her shoulder. There was no hint of forwardness in his touch. On the contrary, the move sent forth only feelings of warmth and unreserved honesty.

"Okay?"

"Okay," she said. "No arguments." She smiled before adding a whispered, "Thank you."

"You're welcome," he said in that deep, liquid voice of his. Then he smiled.

She realized at that moment that the tension knotting her stomach had eased. And she knew he'd worked hard at enabling her to relax.

It wasn't as though her attraction for him had abated. Oh, no. The pale gray summer-weight suit he wore accentuated his tanned complexion. His pristine white shirt was a perfect backdrop for the magenta geometric shapes on his tie. The smell of his cologne was intoxicating. Her desire to be touched and kissed by him burned like a bright, hot fire inside her. And she could easily read a mirrored craving in his eyes, but at the same time she could see that he intended to hold his urges at bay. She didn't know why he'd decided to do so, but she was thankful for his consideration.

Since he seemed determined to contain his ardent feelings, and he also emanated a friendly, openheartedness, she thought it might be a good time to broach the subject of Andy's restrictions.

"Joshua..." she began slowly. "*Can* we talk about the list?"

He touched the tip of his finger to his bottom lip, obviously assessing her and the idea of discussing a topic about which he was quite adamant. She was surprised by her lack of anxiety. She would have thought she'd have been scared witless to bring up the restrictions. Whether it was the beautiful moonlight, the calm night air, or just his amiable manner, she didn't know, but something about tonight helped her to remain calm and collected in the face of what might very well turn into an argument.

Finally he nodded and said, "Sure, we can talk about the list."

So there, under the oak tree, with moonlight fingering through the leafy branches, Cassie pleaded Andy's case. She told him how his son wanted so badly to run and play like other children, how Andy had astutely asked if what he'd heard was true and that children sometimes did "grow out of their allergy problems."

"He wants to punt a football, challenge Eric to a race," she passionately explained. "He wants to climb trees. Joshua, Andy wants with all his heart to be a normal eight-year-old boy."

"But he's not a normal eight-year-old," Joshua pointedly observed.

"I know that. Andy knows that, too. We understand there must be restrictions." She braced herself, then looked directly into his eyes. "All he's asking is that the restrictions be . . . necessary."

"Necessary?" His gaze glinted with a sudden harshness. "Are you insinuating that I'm coddling my son?"

She was amazed that his glare didn't make her want to back down one bit. This needed to be said. "I'm saying that Andy's restrictions should be for Andy's benefit. Not yours."

His jaw muscle tensed.

She took his hand from where it rested on her shoulder and held it between both of hers. "Joshua, please don't be angry. I'm only trying to tell you something that Andy hasn't been able to. He loves you and he's afraid he'll disappoint you."

"Disappoint me?" His frown creased the skin directly between his eyes. "He could never disappoint me."

"He doesn't want you to be angry with him," she tried to explain further. "But he does want his life to change. Even a small change will be for the better."

Joshua slipped his hand from hers and leaned forward, bracing his elbows on his knees. He bowed his head, and Cassie knew he was digesting all that she had told him.

Finally he heaved a sigh and lifted his head to stare out across the yard. "Maybe I have been overprotecting Andrew."

She knew this was a momentous admission for him, so she reached out and placed her hand on his jacket sleeve, but remained silent.

"I have good reason." Joshua's deep, quiet timbre was full of emotion. "You see, I—I let my wife die. There were signs. Signs I failed to see. Elizabeth died because I failed to protect her."

Cassie's heart swelled painfully with compassion.

"Joshua, I don't know what happened to Elizabeth. But I've seen you with Andy. And Eric." *And me,* she thought, but prudently left that out. "You're a kind and caring man. I can't believe you would stand by and not do everything in your power to help your wife."

"I did nothing!" His voice turned suddenly and savagely self-critical. "I should have realized that a bottle of fifty aspirin tablets doesn't just disappear in a week. I should have realized she was in pain!"

"A whole bottle of aspirins?" Cassie could hear her own surprise and shock. "Did you ask her about it?"

"She told me she was having some tension headaches," he said. "She assured me it was only stress. And the next time I asked, she put me off with some ridiculous story about having spilled the aspirin bottle into the sink. A story I fell for. I was stupid—"

"It sounds as though Elizabeth was trying to protect you," Cassie offered. "She didn't want you to worry."

"No, she didn't want me to worry," he said. "But less than a week later the tumor in her brain caused her to have a seizure. She was driving at the time. The car went out of control and smashed into a tree." He hesitated a moment before adding, "She died instantly."

"Oh, Joshua," she said, sliding to the edge of the bench. Once again she reached out and took his hand between both of hers. "I'm so sorry."

"The damnedest thing is," he whispered hoarsely, "the tumor was operable."

"How in the world did you find that out?"

"There was a routine autopsy." He shrugged. "And I requested a copy of the report."

Cassie didn't know what to say. It was obvious that his guilt was immense.

He turned his head to gaze at her. "So, now do you understand why I must protect Andrew?"

She wanted to take him in her arms. To soothe his pain and assuage the self-reproach he'd heaped upon himself like a heavy burden.

"Joshua, you didn't know that a tumor was growing in your wife's head," she said quietly. "If you had, you would have done everything you could for her." She squeezed his hand. "Andy isn't going to die." Then she corrected, "Well, he will ... one day. We all have to die. But trying to protect Andy from everything will only ... smother the life out of him."

He leaned back to rest against the ornate wrought-iron seat and rubbed his free hand across his jaw.

"I don't know, Cassie," he said. "I just don't know."

"Andy has his whole life ahead of him," she persisted. "He has to be allowed to find out what things he can do and what things he can't. You need to let him explore his world." She shifted her weight. "He can start slow. He knows there are very specific things he must stay away from. Eggs and wheat. Cut grass. But with regard to exercise, he needs to find out how much is too much."

He didn't speak, only looked at her with those dark, intense eyes of his.

"Have I overstepped my bounds?" she asked.

For a long time she thought he wasn't going to answer. But then he shook his head.

"No," he said. "I realize that you're only concerned for Andrew. And I appreciate that." He inhaled slowly and withdrew his hand from hers. "And deep down inside, I know you're right."

She felt a tremendous sense of accomplishment, but she only let a tiny smile of triumph touch her lips.

"I'll talk to him tomorrow," he said.

Her smile broadened. "He'll be so happy."

She scooted back and stretched her bare feet out in front of her, reveling in a deep sense of satisfaction that seemed to swell inside her as though the emotion were warm water and she a dry sponge.

"Cassie?" His timbre was deep, liquid.

"Hmm?"

"Tell me what you're afraid of."

She thought her heart would stop beating right then. "Afraid?" she asked, fervently hoping her quavery tone didn't expose her feigned innocence. "What do I have to be afraid of?"

"Oh, Cassie, come on. We're both intelligent people."

She knew very well to what he was referring, just as well as she knew he was staring at her in the dark, but she refused to acknowledge the subject he broached or his steady gaze.

"It's late, Joshua," she said, darting a cursory glance at her watch. "I need to go in."

His quelling hand on her arm stopped her attempt to rise. The feel of his fingers on her skin was like heaven.

"Cassie."

Steeling herself, she lifted her face to gaze at him. His dark eyes held a mixture of gentleness and entreaty that melted away her reserve.

"Please," he said, "talk to me."

"Joshua, I don't know what you want me to say. I don't know what you want from me—"

"Just talk to me," he said. "Is that too much to ask? Stop hiding from me. Spend some time with me. That's all I ask. Give this...spark...or attraction... or whatever it is we're feeling a chance. You know you feel it. It's impossible to deny."

Yes, she felt it all right. And she hated this fear that gripped her so tightly—this fear that battled fiercely with her desire to be with him, to talk to him, to listen to him.

Slowly she turned to him, knowing she must respond, yet scared witless that she'd reveal too much. Silently she sent a quick prayer heavenward for the strength to tell him how she was feeling and for the control that would keep her from going too far.

"Joshua..." She hesitated long enough to take a deep breath. "I told you before that I won't deny that there's something there. Between us, I mean."

She felt flustered, all hot and cold at the same time, sitting here in the romantic moonlight under a canopy of brilliant stars. How could she admit in one breath that she felt something for him and then turn right around and tell him she had no intention of responding to those feelings? She didn't know, but she had to do it. She just had to.

"I simply can't . . . react to it."

His eyes were so intense they nearly swallowed her up.

"But why?" he asked. "Tell me why you don't want to react."

"I didn't say I didn't want to." Heat suffused her face as she made the impetuous statement. "I said," she went on, her voice barely a whisper, "that I can't. I do have some natural . . . urges . . . where you're concerned. But that doesn't mean I have to give in to them."

It was his turn to hesitate. Then he once again asked simply, "Why?"

She didn't trust herself to answer, so she merely sat there and silently watched him watching her.

"I'd never do anything to hurt you," he said. "I mean, if you've been hurt in the past and you're afraid that I'd . . ."

She let him know he was on the wrong track by closing her eyes and shaking her head firmly.

"Well, whatever your fear, we can work it out—"

"No, we can't," she said adamantly. "I've made it a rule never, ever to become intimately involved with an employer."

She was lying through her teeth, but the subject had never had a chance to enter her mind before now and it did sound like a good rule, given the circumstances.

"I'm not asking for intimate involvement." His tone was grave. "I just want . . . I just . . ."

Cassie couldn't stand it, she had to ask. "You just want what?"

"I want to spend some time with you," he said. "No strings attached. And with no expectations of any kind." Then his fingers tightened on her forearm. "I've been invited to a cocktail party Saturday night. Go with me."

She couldn't seem to respond. She knew she should refuse him flat out. But part of her wanted this—a part of her wanted to be with him. Badly.

Her inhalation was shaky, and confusion rocked her to her very foundation. Maybe, she thought, if she understood this spark or attraction or whatever it was that was drawing them together so strongly, then she could deal with it a little less emotionally.

"I need to ask you something." The words had escaped her in an impulsive moment.

"Okay." He released his grip on her arm and rested his elbow behind her on the back of the seat.

She could hardly believe she was about to ask him the question that had been nagging at her since "the experiment" had occurred.

"The other night at the pool," she began, "you said that you had never wanted a woman the way you want me. I wondered how that could be when you were married? What about . . . Elizabeth, your wife?"

Joshua was quiet for a long moment—a moment during which she thought she read several emotions in his dark eyes: sadness, regret and a twinge of guilt. Knowing that she'd precipitated the recall of these obviously troubling feelings in him made her sorry she'd raised the issue.

Finally he tilted his head to one side and smiled tenderly. "You're right, I did say that. And I meant it."

She didn't want to feel it and knew in fact that she shouldn't, but his words, his tone, the look in his gaze, filled her with a sense of pure toe-tingling joy.

"Let me tell you about my marriage to Elizabeth," he said.

"No, please," she rushed to say. "I shouldn't have asked. Your marriage is none of my business."

"Cassie, it's okay. I want to tell you."

A sudden anxiety had gripped her stomach when he offered an explanation, but his candid tone melted it, and it was gone almost before she felt it.

Once more he gazed off over the yard and contemplated his thoughts for a few seconds before he spoke. Cassie took that time to surreptitiously survey him.

So late in the day, his jaw was shadowed by a new growth of stubble. It gave him a rugged look, and she wanted desperately to reach out and smooth her palm across his cheek.

Just then he reached up and rubbed his fingers along his jawline. And her eyes became riveted to his hand. She was surprised by the tanned strength of it, especially when she knew, as a university professor, he must perform little manual labor. His fingers were long and lean, and she remembered how wonderful it had felt as they'd touched her face.

"There was never a time—"

She nearly jumped at the sound of his voice, and realized just how engrossed she'd become in merely looking at him.

"When I don't remember having Elizabeth be a part of my life," he said. "You see, our parents were the best of friends." He looked at her and rested his arm along the back of the seat behind her. "Elizabeth and I grew up together. We learned to ride bikes together, we went to grade school together. Both of us were in-troverts—bookish, intelligent—outcasts."

He hesitated over the adjectives and the last word was accompanied by a frown. Cassie felt an over-whelming desire to lift her hand and smooth away the tiny creases between his thick-lashed eyes.

"We were such good friends, Elizabeth and I," he said. "We continued on through college together." One shoulder rose in a shrug. "It seemed only logical at the time for us to get married."

"Is everything you do logical?" she asked.

He chuckled suddenly. "If I think back over my life, it certainly seems that way."

She remembered the loving relationship her own parents had shared, and how her mother had pined so for her father after he'd died. Was it possible for a woman to love a man so much that she couldn't live without him? She knew the answer to that question was yes.

Absorbed in her own painful memories now, she didn't see the meditative expression with which Joshua studied her.

"But this . . ." he muttered, breaking into her mus-ings by gently touching her hair. "This is anything but logical."

Cassie instantly realized that the "this" he was referring to was the attraction that hummed between them. She knew she should jump up and run into the house, run from the magnetic pull that urged her to lean against the palm of his hand that was so softly stroking the strands of her hair.

Heeding that silent voice of warning in her head, she did jump up from the seat. But she didn't run. Not only didn't she run, she found herself saying the most outrageous thing.

"Well, then, logic be damned," she blurted. "I'd love to go to the party with you."

Chapter Seven

Saturday morning dawned bright, clear and warm. After a quick shower, Cassie dressed in a white sleeveless blouse, a short denim skirt and white canvas sneakers. Her spirits were soaring as she trotted downstairs to the kitchen to fix breakfast.

Today was going to be a big day. First Joshua was planning to take her and the boys to the mall, and then tonight...

Tonight Cassie would be spending the evening with Joshua. A real, live date, she thought, pulling from the refrigerator a carton of orange juice, one of milk, several large grapefruit and a bunch of plump, juicy grapes. The very idea of a date with Joshua made her stomach jump with giddy nerves.

But if the two of you become too involved—

Cassie shut out the silent, ominous echo, just as she'd successfully shut it out for the past few days. She simply closed her eyes and remembered his words. *Whatever your fear, we can work it out.*

As she arranged the fruit on a platter, she let the memory of his words take her, yet again, into the realm of fantasy—a sunny, cheerful world where Joshua never hesitated to kiss her; on the shoulder, the neck, the lips. A world where she could feel free to run her fingers through his hair or rub his shoulders after he'd had a long, hard day in the laboratory. A world where she fixed breakfast, not for the professor, his son, and her brother, but for her *family*.

This was a fantasy that had been ruminating in her head ever since the night Joshua had asked her to the party. Something had happened to her that night. Some sort of wild abandon had taken over her rational senses, and her fantasy had been born. Her creation had slowly taken shape, and with each passing day, her dream had become more involved.

Oh, she realized it for what it was. But did it hurt to ask herself, *what if? What if* she could keep her past from Joshua? *What if* he wanted her so much that he never thought to ask her silly questions about her background?

He wanted her, of that she was certain. And the idea alone thrilled her beyond measure. She made a trip to the dining room table with glasses and drinks and then went back into the kitchen, refusing to think of what tomorrow would bring. She didn't want to think beyond tonight. Tonight would be . . . wonderful.

"Good morning."

Cassie glanced toward the doorway and saw Joshua.

"Hi," she said, noticing how his green knit shirt hugged his broad chest. His beige twill shorts showed off lean, muscular thighs. He looked so different, so outdoorsy in these casual clothes.

He came across the kitchen, pulled a grape from the vine and popped it into his mouth. She busied herself with slicing the bagels and lining them up on the broiling pan, but she didn't fail to notice the intense, vibrant energy that pulsated in the room.

He leaned his hip against the counter and asked, "So, is the shopping trip still on this morning?"

"Oh, yes," she said. She opened the oven door and popped the bagels under the broiler. "The boys were so excited last night, they could hardly get to sleep."

"I'm sorry I was so late coming in last night," he said. "I had to finish up a few things in the lab so that I'd have this morning free. I'll have to go in for a couple of hours this afternoon, but this morning belongs to you, Andrew and Eric."

For some reason, his words made her go all warm inside. She didn't know what to say, so she didn't say anything.

At that moment the boys bounded into the kitchen.

"Are we goin' now?"

"Is it time to go?"

Both boys spoke at once.

"Whoa, there," Cassie said. "Up to the table for breakfast first."

"Aw-ww!"

"Now." Joshua joined in Cassie's cause. "Eat first, shop later."

Cassie guided Eric into the dining room and he slipped into his chair. He took a big gulp of the milk his sister poured for him.

"Am I really going to get a new mitt?" He whispered the question so that only Cassie could hear.

The excitement and anticipation twinkling in his eyes nearly made her cry. The milky mustache smeared above his upper lip nearly made her laugh.

Smiling warmly, she nodded her assurance.

"I'll be right back," she told the boys. "I have to get the bagels."

Back in the kitchen, she saw that Joshua had taken the pan from the oven and was putting the toasted bagels on a plate.

"You shouldn't have to do that," she said, hurrying across the room.

"I don't mind."

She reached for the plate at the same moment he did. Their fingers entangled as they grasped the rim of the plate. The current of that touch sent shock waves jolting through her. Her eyes sought and found his.

His gaze expressed an open affection the strength of which nearly knocked her to her knees. His freshly shaven face was so handsome, she could have stared at him all day long. A hint of his cologne only intensified the feeling. In that instant she wanted to reach out and smooth her fingertips across his sensual mouth, lean over the plate of bagels and kiss him.

She blinked twice, her tongue darting out to moisten her cotton-dry lips. The desire she felt was showing in her eyes, on her face, in the set of her body—she was certain of it. But she felt helpless to stop it, because it seemed as though the fantasy she'd spent the past few days creating was somehow getting caught up in the reality of right now.

With his free hand, he caught her chin between his thumb and the knuckle of his index finger. "I know how you're feeling," he said, his voice sounding on the edge of control. "I'm feeling the same."

They stood there for a long breathless moment, and Cassie realized that he was waiting for a sign, some signal from her as to whether he could move forward or if she wanted him to back off.

God, how she wanted him to make that decision on his own! Because she knew if he were to go with his feelings, he would surely kiss her. But he was too much of a gentleman to choose for her.

Slowly, after much silent deliberation, she came to understand that she was not yet ready to cross that unseen line that would take her ever so close to her fantasy world. She lowered her gaze.

"The boys are waiting." Her tone was coarse with regret and she knew he heard it.

With utmost courtesy, he remained silent and pulled away from her. She didn't know if there was disappointment showing on his features because she couldn't bring herself to look at his face.

Breakfast was a rushed affair as Andy and Eric chattered away about the prospective shopping trip. Afterward, she sent them upstairs to make their beds and clean up their rooms while she loaded the dishwasher and put away the leftover fruit and juice.

Joshua went out to pull the car out of the garage, and after he'd gone, Cassie felt an unmistakable emptiness in the room that filled her with a fresh sense of regret that she'd let the intimate moment before breakfast pass her by.

* * *

The boys hadn't stopped talking the entire way to the mall, they'd bounced from one topic to another. Cassie was relieved that their innocent bantering had kept all four of them occupied and held at bay that awkward tension she'd expected.

They entered the main entrance directly across from the sporting goods store. Eric and Andy rushed ahead.

"I've never seen Andrew so excited about anything," Joshua said.

"Eric, too." She snared his gaze with serious eyes. "I can't tell you what this means to him. He's never had—"

"I want to do it," he insisted lightly, as he propelled her into the store with a hand placed at the small of her back.

The next half hour was spent examining gloves of various shapes and sizes. The saleswoman relayed a variety of information regarding every aspect of a baseball glove: leather versus manmade material, a solid cup versus interlaced webbing, hand-sewn versus machine-made. Cassie never knew there were so many things to consider when purchasing a baseball mitt.

Finally the boys made their choices. Joshua allowed them to pick out a new baseball and they all went to the register to pay for the items.

"It's been such a pleasure to wait on you," the saleswoman commented as she punched buttons on the computerized register. "We don't usually see the whole family come in."

Cassie froze.

The woman addressed the boys. "I've never seen brothers look so different from one another."

Darting a glance at the boys, Cassie was surprised by the pure glee written on both their faces at having been mistakenly identified as brothers.

Pointing at Andy, the saleswoman said, "With your red hair and dark eyes, you look just like your father." Then she turned her attention to Eric. "And you look like your mother."

Cassie felt she should set the woman straight, but was too startled to say a word.

The woman smiled first at Joshua and then at Cassie. "You two must be very proud of your little family."

"We certainly are."

Joshua's response flowed from him like a smooth-running stream. With a quiet, quick inhalation, Cassie jerked her gaze to him. The most charming, teasing glint lit his eyes.

She looked from Joshua to Eric to Andy. The three of them were truly enjoying being mistaken as a family unit. Cassie wished she, too, could enjoy the situation, but this was too, too close to the fantasy she'd conjured. The scene made her ill at ease.

The saleswoman handed Joshua his change and his receipt. She put the gloves in separate bags and held them out to the boys.

"Thanks," Eric said. He looked up at Joshua. "Thank you, too."

"Yeah, Dad," Andy chimed in. "Thanks!"

As they went out of the mall into the warm, sunny day, Joshua suggested, "Let's go to the park and you two can try out your new gloves."

The boys cheered their approval.

"Cassie?" Joshua raised his brows inquiringly.

"Sure," she said. "But, Andy, you'll need to let me know if you begin to feel ill or you have trouble breathing. Do you have your inhaler?"

"Right here." Andy patted his pocket.

Joshua parked the car and the four of them found an out-of-the-way spot that was open and flat. The boys distanced themselves from each other and Eric tossed his ball to Andy.

Cassie's heart swelled when she heard the sound of the boys' laughter. It was so good to see them playing outdoors in the fresh air and wide, open spaces.

Glancing at Joshua, she noticed how intently he watched his son, a frown of concentration knitting his brow.

"It's okay," she tried to assure him. "We'll watch him closely. Come sit down on the bench."

"We probably shouldn't stay long," he said.

"I agree," she said, settling herself on the wooden bench. "But Andy's so excited to be here."

"Yes. And that excitement alone could cause an asthma attack."

The stress in his tone prompted her to reach out and touch his forearm. "We'll watch him closely," she repeated gently.

He didn't respond. When she made to pull her hand away, he stopped her by placing his hand on top of hers.

"I'm sorry, Cassie," he said. "I'm just not used to this. Andrew is usually safe and sound at the house. I never had to worry about him..." He let his statement trail off and sighed deeply.

"Well..." Cassie began hesitantly "...you may have thought you had nothing to worry about, but..."

"But what?"

She darted a glance at Andy some distance away and she reluctantly came to a decision. Turning back to Joshua, she lowered her tone so that only he could hear, and relayed the events of her first meeting with Andy—up in the tree with the kitten.

"Andrew was up in that tree?" Joshua asked, incredulity clearly expressed in his features. "With a cat?"

Cassie could only nod.

"But he's allergic to cats," he said. "He knows better. You should have told me. I would have—"

"Now don't get angry," she pleaded. "I talked to him and he knows he made a mistake. The only reason I told you about it is because it's normal for a young child to test his limits. Wouldn't you rather loosen his reins a little and be aware of what he's doing than let him continue to test his limits on his own?"

Joshua watched his son toss the baseball to Eric, who just missed catching it. Lifting his hand, Joshua rubbed his fingers across his jaw in contemplation.

She sensed his dark eyes on her and she directed her gaze to his, waiting for his response.

"You're right," he murmured. Then he shook his head ruefully. "But I'm going to need some help."

Without hesitation, Cassie gently squeezed his arm and smiled. "That's why I'm here."

Later that evening Cassie tugged panty hose over the toes, heel, ankle and calf of first one leg, then the other. She smoothed her hand over the sheer nylon material simply out of habit.

What does one wear to a summer cocktail party? she wondered. Before Joshua had left this afternoon to spend some time in his lab at the university, she'd asked him just that question. His response had been, "Upscale casual." She interpreted that to mean not too dressy, yet not too casual. Which left her wondering, What does one wear to a summer cocktail party?

Scowling, she inspected the clothes hanging in her closet and muttered, "You didn't help a bit, Joshua."

The little black skirt she pulled out was years and years old, but the A-line design made it timeless. And Cassie decided her royal blue blouse would look nice with the skirt. The blouse wasn't made of silk, but the soft rayon was clingy and flattering.

She slipped her feet into royal blue heels that she'd purchased at a discount outlet last summer and then stood in front of the mirror to scrutinize how she looked.

The bold blue color of her blouse accentuated her blue eyes. A little mascara only added to the effect. She brushed her hair until it shone with glossy highlights and decided at the last minute not to pin it up but to let it swing freely down her back.

As she placed the hairbrush on the dresser, she let her mind rove over the wonderful morning she'd spent with Joshua and the boys. The four of them *had* been like a real family.

Her insides had felt all fuzzy and warm as she'd sat on the park bench with Joshua and watched the boys play. Soon, though, Andy had enticed his father to participate. Cassie had sat there only a few moments before she, too, decided to join in the fun. The couple of hours they'd spent at the park had been as close to heaven as Cassie had ever been.

And here she was about to step out onto the clouds of heaven again. A night out with Joshua. The mere thought made her skin go all prickly.

She concentrated on applying a light coat of lipstick to her lips and then went to check on the boys.

Hearing their murmured voices in Andy's room, she knocked on his door and then opened it. The boys looked up from a comic book they'd been discussing.

"Are you two all ready for bed?" she asked, but she could plainly see that both boys were wearing their pajamas.

"It's nearly time for me to go," she told them. "Joshua should be home soon. While he changes his clothes, I'm going to drive over and pick up Mary, so you two won't be alone."

"Aw-ww," Eric lamented. "We're too big for a baby-sitter."

Cassie grinned. "Don't think of it as a night with a baby-sitter. Think of it as a visit with Mary."

The boys exchanged a pained look that had her chuckling. "You two better be good," she cautioned.

She heard the front door open and her stomach flip-flopped as she hurried down the stairs. "Hi," she said.

Joshua smiled at her and Cassie felt bombarded by an energy force strong enough to brighten the lights in the room.

"I stopped on my way home and picked up Aunt Mary," he said. "I thought I'd save you a trip."

How considerate of him, she thought, then realized that she hadn't even noticed Mary standing there by the door.

"Mary, how are you?" she asked, hurrying to take the older woman's coat.

"I'm doing great," Mary said. "I'm happy to be able to spend some time with the boys."

"Well, I'm going to run upstairs and take a quick shower." Joshua nodded to his aunt and threw Cassie a quick wink before he left the room.

Cassie spent the next twenty minutes or so dodging Mary's gently probing questions. How could she explain to Mary how she felt about Joshua when she didn't know herself? If she even attempted to verbalize the physical aspects of how she desired him, or the intense attraction that seemed to literally pull them together—why, the older woman would probably keel over in a swoon. Dodging Mary's questions, at least for the time being, was her only option.

When Joshua entered the living room, she turned to face him with every intention of smiling. But at the sight of him—his freshly shaven face, his brown eyes glinting with anticipation, his wavy red hair still damp from his shower—she could only stare silently.

"Is something wrong?" he asked, a look of concern shadowing his features.

"Wrong?" Her voice sounded breathless and weak as she wondered, *What could be wrong with someone so utterly perfect in every way?* Shrugging one shoulder, she stated frankly, "Nothing's wrong. It's just that you look so...good."

She let her eyes travel the length of him. His navy blazer hugged his shoulders provocatively and went nicely with his tawny-colored trousers. His white dress shirt and navy print silk tie would have looked mundane and ordinary on any other man, but he filled it out in such a way that it made her want to loosen the tie and unfasten the shirt buttons to see what pleasures were hidden beneath.

Then she heard him chuckle—a low, seductive sound vibrating from deep in his chest. She couldn't stop her face from flaming; not because of what she'd said to him, which was the honest truth, but from what she'd thought.

"It's nice to be appreciated," he said. One corner of his mouth turned up in a grin. "And I didn't mention it before, but you look . . . good, too."

The way he said the word *good,* along with the look in his eyes, told her he really thought she looked better than good—much better. She smiled, gazing at him almost invitingly. Her tongue darted to moisten her lips. Suddenly she realized she was actually flirting with this man. And enjoying herself immensely.

"Why don't you two get on your way?"

Cassie nearly gasped aloud when Mary spoke. Heaven above, this little byplay between herself and Joshua had put Mary completely out of Cassie's mind.

"That's a good idea," Joshua said. "Cassie?"

She stood and, without hesitation, took Joshua's outreached hand.

"I've already said good-night to the boys," he told her. Then he turned to Mary. "We won't be too late."

"Please," Mary stressed. "Take your time."

Joshua opened the car door for Cassie and she hesitated before getting inside. Gazing up at him in the moonlight, she touched the tips of her fingers to the back of his hand where it rested on the top of the door.

"I want to thank you for asking me to the party tonight," she said, her tone conveying the candor she felt. "You know I was a little hesitant about accepting, but I'm glad I did."

"So am I."

His mouth pulled back in the barest of smiles and the golden flecks of his deep brown eyes danced with an anticipation that made Cassie's heart thump wildly under her rib cage.

"We're going to have a good time tonight," he promised.

She thanked the stars twinkling overhead that the drive to the party would be short. Joshua had told her that the host of the party lived barely five miles away, near Stringer's Pond.

The air in the close confines of the car was thick with some unnameable emotion. Well, unnameable wasn't exactly correct; Cassie knew what it was that had the air so dense she could hardly breathe, but she wasn't yet ready to face the sheer sensuality that pulled at every fibre of her being.

Joshua turned onto Pond Circle, the narrow road that looped the small, irregular-shaped pond. When he pulled to the side of the road and cut the engine, her gaze swung around, questioning him.

"Do you mind—" he looked toward the water and then back at her "—if we take a little walk by the pond?" His face took on a sheepish expression as he continued. "I'd like to enjoy a few minutes alone with you before I have to share your company with all those others."

She was relieved that the dark interior of the car hid her face because she was certain that his charming flattery caused her cheeks to tinge with heat. "I'd like that," she told him.

They met at the front of the car and Joshua held out his hand to her. She took it as though it were the most natural thing in the world. And when she found it difficult to walk in heels across the uneven grassy ground, he offered her his arm, and she moved closer, hugging his biceps to her.

The moonlight reflected on the water in a long, wavering trail of brightness against a dark, murky background. The frogs croaked an erratic song and the pussy willows were nearly motionless in the calm night air.

"It's beautiful," she whispered, unwilling to have her voice spoil this perfect setting.

"I agree." Joshua clasped his hand over hers. "I wanted to build a house out here . . ."

The way he'd let the sentence trail sparked her curiosity and she asked, "Why didn't you?"

He gave her a sidelong glance. "You'll laugh at me." Then he said, "Elizabeth thought it wasn't a logical thing to do. We were settled in a house, why upset everyone to move just five miles away?"

He waited for her to chuckle, and when she didn't, he did.

"Since I've spent time with you," he said, "I've noticed just how ordered and rational my existence has been."

Cassie didn't laugh because it struck her as kind of melancholic that he might have given up something he truly wanted rather than "upset" his family—mainly his wife. Still, she didn't want him to feel regret about how he'd lived his life.

"Order and rationality aren't terrible things," she acknowledged.

"Yes, but if you choose reason and logic, then you can't have excitement and spontaneity. You end up living a life that's very ordered but . . . rather dull."

She stopped in her tracks and looked up at him. "Joshua, that sounds so sad."

"But that's what I like about you," he said. "You do the unexpected. You're impulsive and fun-loving—"

She bristled a little at his description. "You make me sound like an airhead."

"No, no, no," he hurried to say. "That's not what I meant at all. Here, sit down a minute." He led her to a huge, ancient fallen tree, years of use as a bench having smoothed the surface to a satiny finish. Pulling out a handkerchief, he laid it out for her to sit on.

Even though she felt affronted by his words, she couldn't help but notice his gallant behavior. Offering her his handkerchief so she wouldn't get her skirt dirty was a small gesture, but Cassie had never had someone about whom she felt so strongly treat her so much like a lady.

He settled beside her, straddling the log. "What I meant was," he said, "you're so capable, so competent, yet at the same time you're full of spirit." He laughed softly. "I mean, who else but you would climb a tree in your Sunday best right before a job interview?"

He did have a point, she had to admit. Giving him a wry grin, she remarked, "But I did have a logical reason for doing so."

His fingers gently caught her jaw and he gazed into her eyes. "You certainly did," he whispered.

As he searched her face, she was overwhelmed by the emotions clamoring deep in the pit of her belly. His touch was like a switch that turned on a churn inside her. He was going to kiss her, she just knew it. Dear God, she *hoped* he was going to kiss her.

"I like you, Cassie Simmons," he said. "I like you a lot." The husky quality of his voice sent sexy shivers to course over her skin.

"I like you, too," she murmured.

They moved closer to one another, and finally surrendered to the powerful magnetic attraction that had been pulling at them ever since the first time they'd met.

His lips were warm, smooth and moist when they touched hers. Brushed would have been a better description, because she'd barely felt it before she heard his almost painful exhalation and felt him pull her against him in a hug.

"You feel so good in my arms," he whispered against her ear, smoothing his hands over her back. "You smell so good. Like summer wildflowers."

He pressed his lips on the tender skin behind her ear and slowly, deliberately, moved down her neck. His kisses left little seared spots in their wake. Cassie thought she'd die from the heat, but found herself tilting her head to the side to offer him more of her flesh to kiss. And he did—to the point where she found herself holding back a desire-induced groan.

She felt his thumb graze the tender underside of her breast. Her breath caught in her throat when her nipples drew into tight buds of yearning. She gulped in air and slid her hands up over his arms and shoulders.

He may think her capable, or adept, or whatever adjectives he'd used—her fogged brain couldn't remember exactly—but right now she wanted to toss away every trace of logic and act on what she was feeling. Then the blood pounding in her ears drowned out all thought, and she did act.

Catching his hand in hers, she guided it to cup her breast. His sharp intake of breath did nothing to deter her, it only spurred her on.

"Cassie." Her name came from him in a ragged rush.

She reached up and framed his face between her palms. After gazing at him for one hot, frantic moment, she pulled his mouth to hers.

The intimate contact scorched her lips and she welcomed the heat. Simultaneously his thumb trailed across her breast and she parted her lips in an invitation for him to deepen the kiss.

His tongue plundered the soft recesses of her mouth and she greeted him happily. A thought filtered through her hazy mind; she should feel wanton and ashamed of her behavior, but she didn't. This only felt . . . right.

She slid her hands through his thick, wavy hair and entwined her fingers at the back of his head. She didn't want this to end, she didn't want him to escape.

When she took his bottom lip between her teeth, he

groaned, and Cassie felt excitement and pleasure burst through her knowing she'd caused this reaction in him.

His hand slid to her hip and he pulled her against him tightly. It was when she felt the hard length of his desire pressing against her that rational thought began to return.

She pulled back, her eyes wide.

He rubbed the pad of his thumb over her swollen lips. "I'm sorry," he said softly. "I shouldn't have done that. But I needed you to understand how you affect me."

Mortification flooded her and she tried to avert her gaze, but he refused to let her. He tilted her chin up and looked directly into her eyes.

"Don't be embarrassed," he pleaded. "I enjoyed it just as much as you." A soft chuckle emanated from deep in his throat. "Probably more than you."

She shook her head dolefully. "I'm not so sure."

He laughed again and she was able to smile.

"We better get ourselves to the party," he said.

Cassie felt as if she floated all the way back to the car.

Chapter Eight

Cassie arrived at the party on Joshua's arm, enveloped in a hazy ecstasy that made her feel like a princess in some enchanted fairy tale.

Nathan Melrath, the host of the party, welcomed her warmly. And as he and Joshua exchanged greetings, Cassie took a moment to scan the room.

The house had an open, airy feel. She could see the living room and dining room from where she stood. The far wall held a patio door that was open and several people were out on a redwood deck. A slow, sensuous jazz tune softly filled in the background of several simultaneous and boisterous conversations of a dozen or so smartly dressed men and women. Ice tinkling against crystal glasses, spurts of laughter, the intriguing smell of hors d'oeuvres were clear evidence that a successful social gathering was well under way.

The first hairline fissure in Cassie's euphoric facade came with the introductions. Don, Carol, Susan, Henry, Janice, Vincent, another Susan, William. Heaven above, she'd never remember all these names, and the thought brought a moment of sheer panic that tensed every muscle in her body.

As though sensing her apprehension, Joshua smiled down at her and squeezed her hand reassuringly.

"Don't worry," he said. "You'll get to know everyone eventually."

He's right, she told herself. She plastered on a smile and tried to retreat into the foggy Eden she'd come in the door with.

"Let me get you something to drink," he said.

"A little white wine would be nice," she told him.

She moved farther into the living room as she watched him disappear into what she suspected was the kitchen. She felt desperately alone in the crowded room.

A woman approached her and Cassie felt her insides freeze. Was the woman's name Susan? Or Carol? Cassie couldn't remember, and nervous anxiety made the little hairs on the back of her neck stand up, but she tried to smile anyway.

"So, Cassie," the woman said. "Joshua's never brought a date to one of these things." She swooped out her hand to indicate the party going on behind her. "How did the two of you meet?"

"I'm Joshua's nanny."

She realized her mistake at the same instant the woman smirked.

"Not...not Joshua's nanny, actually," she stuttered, feeling her face redden. "I work for Joshua as Andy's nanny."

The woman's brows raised. "A nanny. How... sweet."

"Susan, can I slip into this conversation?" a middle-aged blond woman asked as she joined them.

"Oh, Jill," Susan almost purred, "have you met Cassie?"

As Cassie shook Jill's hand, Susan continued. "She's Joshua's baby-sitter."

"Nanny." Cassie murmured the correction.

"You two should have a few things in common," Susan said, not even trying to mask the condescending smile that slid across her face. "You know—crayons, Tinkertoys, carpools. It's hell raising children."

With that parting remark, Susan sauntered away toward the dining room.

"Don't let her bother you," Jill advised. "Susan is like a great white that hasn't fed in days."

Cassie gave a shaky smile and tried to laugh, but the sound that came from her was flat and unnatural. "I did feel as though she were circling for the kill."

"That's why I hurried over," Jill said. "She's pretty uppity about who she spends her time with. Since I quit my job several years ago, Susan hasn't given me the time of day. Because I'm not pursuing a career at the moment, Susan thinks I can't put two intelligent words together." She grinned. "I thought, seeing as though you were meeting her for the first time, you might need a little backup."

"I appreciate the support." This time Cassie's smile was genuine.

"So, you're Joshua's nanny?" Jill asked.

There didn't seem to be even a hint of insult in the tone of Jill's voice, so Cassie told her about Andy and Eric. She listened attentively until Cassie had finished.

"Well, as the shark implied, the two of us do have something in common," Jill said. "I have a son. He's five. And he's the joy of my life." Her gaze was level and direct as she added, "He was born with Down's syndrome."

Cassie's smile faded.

"Don't feel sorry for me," she said. "Lee is my pride and joy. I'm happy I gave up my job to be with him every day." Jill glanced over her shoulder toward Susan, and when she turned back, one brow was raised in irritation. "But for *her* to infer that any mindless booby could raise children really burns my butt."

Cassie realized from Jill's tone just how annoyed she'd become.

"Crayons and carpools," Jill mumbled. "I guess it's time for me to *re*remind Susan that my master's doesn't become null and void simply because I choose not to use it at this point in my life."

At that moment Joshua joined them and handed Cassie a delicate crystal glass half filled with white wine.

"Here you are," he said to Cassie. Smiling at Jill, he said, "How are you this evening?"

"Humph," Jill grumbled. "You should know better than to leave a newcomer alone in these shark-infested waters." She turned on her heel and headed toward the dining room.

Cassie directed her gaze at Joshua and nearly laughed at the confusion written on his handsome face.

"What was that all about?" he asked.

"It's nothing," Cassie said. She didn't want him worrying about her. "Jill just let herself get worked up about something Susan said."

"Oh?" It was evident from his interested look that he wanted to know more.

A gentleman across the room hailed Joshua by calling his name and Cassie felt relieved for the interruption.

"I should go over there and talk to Garrett," Joshua told her. "We have an ongoing argument concerning the pros and cons of university research." He grinned. "I'm pro, he's con. You want to join us?"

Cassie shook her head. "You go. I'll be okay."

"You'll mingle?"

"Oh, yes," she promised in a voice filled with false brightness.

She stood there a moment and watched Joshua's broad back as he crossed the room. God, but he was gorgeous. And he had a body firm with sinewy muscle. She could easily recall the feel of his hard arms and shoulders as he'd embraced her—could easily remember his hot, moist kiss.

Cassie took a deep breath to calm the pounding of her heart. The wine tasted light and fruity as it traveled over her tongue and down her throat. She tipped the glass for another swallow, never taking her eyes off Joshua's exquisite profile.

Why am I so attracted to him? she wondered, not for the first time. She knew his handsome face and dark, wavy hair were enough to turn any woman's head. But there was more to Joshua that she found compelling. He was a kind and loving father, compassionate and understanding. And he was a deep thinker. He was smart.

It was the scholarly quality about him that intrigued her most of all, she was certain. Joshua was all the things she wished she could be. No matter what she and Eric and Andy talked about, Joshua always seemed to know something about the topic. Cassie found Joshua's intellect extremely . . . sexy.

He glanced her way, then back at the man he was talking to. A moment later he did a double take, and that's when she remembered she'd promised him she'd mingle. She nodded in response to his querying look in an effort to ease his worried frown.

Looking around the room, she swallowed with difficulty. Her throat felt dry as cotton as she nervously considered which group of people to approach. She took a tiny sip of wine, its soothing warmth giving her some much needed strength. There were small clusters of two, three, and sometimes four people in the living and dining rooms. There were several others out on the wooden patio beyond the wide, open glass doors, and when the door to the kitchen swung open, she could see at least two people socializing there.

Straightening her shoulders, she moved toward the closest group. But when she heard the phrase "in vitro drug metabolism," her heart started to hammer. The only *in vitro* she'd ever read about had to do with fertility—helping a woman become pregnant. But *drug metabolism?* What did that mean? How could she contribute to a discussion on a subject of which she'd never heard? She didn't bother to stop, but simply quickened her steps straight through the dining room and pushed open the door to the kitchen.

"Hi, Cassie."

"I've just come for a refill, Nathan," she said, relieved that she remembered the host's name.

"Help yourself."

Putting more concentration into filling her glass than was necessary, Cassie kept one ear on what Nathan was saying to the young gentleman opposite him.

"That's where an energy-conversion photometer comes into play," Nathan remarked.

Cassie's nervous anxiety forced her to cast a sidelong glance at the younger man. His naive excitement was blatant evidence that he was a graduate student rather than a teacher.

"I learned about that in my freshman year," the young man said. "Let me see if I remember. A photometer converts the radiant energy of stars, right?"

"Yes, the conversion is made into a more measurable form of energy—"

"Electricity," the young man eagerly provided.

"Exactly," Cassie heard as she left the kitchen and retraced her steps through the dining room.

She hesitated only long enough to hear the word "ethnocentrism" from one group, and the phrase "post-modernist bourgeois liberal" from the other before she decided to flee toward the patio doors.

As she passed Joshua, he reached out and captured her wrist without halting his argument.

"But without university research," he said to Garrett, "there would never have been the discovery of the gene that predisposes a certain percentage of the population to colon cancer." He lifted one hand in an effort to emphasis his point. "You must agree that research is a benefit to society."

"But it *must* be left to private industry," Garrett debated heatedly. "Colleges and universities must keep education their primary concern."

"Cassie, can you believe what he's saying?" Joshua asked her.

Panic rose like bile in her throat. She tried to smile, but failed miserably. Finally she shook her head in answer. Then she whispered, "I'm going to step outside, if you don't mind."

Without missing a beat, Joshua turned back to the man and said, "Education *is* the primary concern, and you know it. And private industry is too focused on the profit margin..."

The night air was warm and still, and Cassie moved to a deserted side of the patio. She closed her eyes and inhaled the delicate scent of summer, but she could find no solace in the blessed moment of solitude or the flowery fragrance of the air.

Dear God in Heaven, what was she doing here? How could she possibly have tricked herself into believing she could hold her own with Joshua's peers? These were educated people. People who had fancy degrees and important careers.

"Cassie."

Cassie froze and felt a painful wrenching in her gut when she recognized Susan's sly tone. Slowly she turned and saw the woman suck deeply on a cigarette.

After she exhaled, Susan said, "Come give us your opinion. We're discussing *The Scarlet Letter* and

Hawthorne's hidden messages revealing the evil of the human soul."

Cassie wasn't completely stupid. She knew *The Scarlet Letter* was a classic piece of literature, that a great American novelist named Nathaniel Hawthorne wrote it and that it had something to do with an adulterous woman. But she did have to admit she'd never read it.

She probably would have. If she'd stayed in high school.

How could she give any kind of intelligent opinion about a book she'd never even read?

Her smile was jerky, she could feel it. "I'm not feeling well," she said suddenly.

Susan's grin held not one iota of concern. "You don't look well."

"Maybe a walk in the garden will help." Cassie hurried down the steps and rushed out into the safety of the darkness without looking back.

Once in the shadows of the leafy trees, she slowed her pace. The perspiration on her brow felt cool, but she wiped at it with trembling fingers.

The haunting questions came back to torment her. How could she ever have thought she could date Joshua? How could she have seriously believed that she and a man like him could have anything in common? How could she have let herself become involved in this situation?

After walking a few hundred feet, she noticed the heels of her shoes began to sink in the soft and sandy ground. The radiant moonlight glowed on the dark, glassy pond. Cassie wished her emotional state was as calm as the beautiful scene before her.

A fat toad croaked in the marsh reeds, and when Cassie's presence frightened it, it hopped into the pond with a loud splash. She watched the toad as it swam away, the murky water sluicing over its head.

In Joshua's world of radiant moonlight, crystal goblets and intellectual conversation, she was like that toad: all green, bumpy and ugly. She didn't fit in with the people of his circle. Just as most of the people at that party would find that wart-ridden toad distasteful, they found *her* distasteful.

She had nothing in common with those people. Nothing. She couldn't interact with them, couldn't talk with them, couldn't . . . couldn't . . .

The turmoil she felt made her bury her face in the palms of her hands.

Joshua would never want someone who was shunned by his friends. Oh, he wanted her, she knew that. But the attraction he felt for her was only physical. How could it be anything else? She certainly didn't have two brain cells to rub together. And soon, after he'd spent some time with her, he'd see that for himself. She'd be left feeling hurt and humiliated.

How did you ever fool yourself into thinking you could have a relationship with Joshua? she wondered.

It had all started with that statement Joshua had made. "We can work it out," he'd said, implying that there wasn't anything that should stop them from exploring the attraction they felt for one another. She'd actually let herself begin to believe it might be true.

And then there was that shopping trip to the mall where the salesclerk had mistaken them for a real family. The boys had loved it and Joshua had played along, letting Andy and Eric have their fun.

The trip to the park had been the final clincher. They had played together, had laughed together, just like a real family. Cassie had let herself dream that maybe they *could* be a real family.

All these things had lulled her into a sense of hope for the future—a sense of hope that was utterly and totally false.

When Joshua had made that statement, he'd had no idea what he was talking about. No idea! The problem that loomed between them wasn't something as simple as a bad past relationship. The problem between them was like a stone wall that was too wide, too tall and too thick for either one of them to scale.

And this problem wasn't going away. She'd always be a high school dropout. She'd always bear that ugly, horrible scar.

She slid her hands down over her face and pressed her fingers to her lips. How could she have let this happen? That question was sure to drive her mad before this was over. But, she thought again, how could she? How could she let herself fall in love with—

Her eyes grew wide. Dear God in Heaven! She'd fallen in love with Joshua. Her throat convulsed as she dragged air into her lungs. Thoughts whirled through her mind faster than she could comprehend them.

Clenching shut her eyes, she pressed tight fists against her temples to stop the questions, the criticism, and the self-condemnation that raced around in her head.

"You're a fool!" Her harsh whisper carried on the still air over the pond. *A fool,* she silently repeated.

Finally she lowered her arms to her sides, her hands still drawn into fists. Although she stared off over the dark water, she didn't see the scene before her. Her mind became as calm and serene as the pond's glassy surface.

She'd been an idiot to believe that she and Joshua could ever share any kind of relationship besides that of employer and employee. There was no way she could keep her secret from him. And there was no way, once he knew, that he would want to have anything else to do with her. He wouldn't want her taking care of his son, and he wouldn't want her in his personal life.

She needed this job. For Eric's sake.

But even more than that, she needed her pride. Without her self-respect, she'd have nothing. Absolutely nothing.

She must make Joshua believe that she wasn't interested in him in any way except as an employer. But how was she going to do that after the way she'd kissed him so wantonly this evening?

The mere thought of his mouth on hers made her blood heat and race through her veins like liquid lava. No one had ever made her feel so womanly, so sensual.

Rubbing her fingers across her forehead, she banished the image from her mind. She had to set things right. She had to protect Eric. She had to protect herself.

"Cassie?"

She jumped, and couldn't decide whether it was her name breaking the night silence or the sound of Joshua's voice that had startled her more.

NANNY AND THE PROFESSOR 141

"I didn't mean to frighten you," he apologized.

She shook her head. "It's okay," she told him. "I was just thinking of you."

"Oh, yeah?"

The teasing glint in his eye made her heart flip over in her chest. But the memory of her decision to cool things between them was too near, too raw for her to react as she wanted—in kind—so she simply erased all emotion from her face.

Evidently he didn't notice the change in her and he took a step closer, reaching out with both hands to clasp her upper arms.

His lips looked so inviting and he smelled wonderfully woodsy, and his hands on her skin felt warm and strong and secure, but she forced herself to close her eyes for the briefest second so she could block the sensory information that bombarded her brain.

"Joshua." Her voice was a tortured whisper.

His brow wrinkled. "What is it?" he asked. "What's wrong?"

He made to pull her to him, but she stopped him by pressing her palm against his hard chest. "Please," she said. "If you don't mind, I'd like to go home."

The crease between his dark, intense eyes deepened. "You aren't having a good time?"

"It's not that. I'm not feeling well," she lied, and realized immediately that this probably wouldn't be the last one she told him.

"Of course we can go home," he said. "Let's go say our goodbyes—"

"Do we have to?" she asked in a rush. The thought of going back into that house, of facing those people, sent nervous tremors throughout her whole body.

"Well," he said, "I really should thank Nathan...."

"Of course." She nodded. "But, would you say goodbye for me and I'll meet you at the car?"

"Sure." He gave her a quick, reassuring smile before turning back toward the house.

Cassie stood there for several minutes feeling so alone she thought her heart would break right in two. And when she finally did start out toward the car, she purposefully kept a wide distance between herself and the house. Still, she could hear the music, the echoing laughter, and a heavy mantle of humiliation settled over her as though every person at the party knew her disgraceful secret.

As she moved away from the house, she realized that she could never be a part of that kind of life. She would always be on the fringe of such a group of people—never belonging—and the humiliation she felt solidified into a deep sense of sadness. She could almost feel the chasm between Joshua and herself widening with every passing second.

Joshua sat in his study, absently tapping a pencil against the desk top. His mood was as dark and brooding as the gray, overcast afternoon sky. He should be in his laboratory at the university, or at least wading through the pile of essays on his desk waiting to be graded. But Cassie kept intruding on his thoughts.

A week ago she had given him the kiss of a lifetime, all hot and wet and wonderful. A kiss that had made his blood boil. A kiss that, even now as he brought the vivid image to mind, could make his desire for her painfully and physically evident—so evident, in fact, that it was necessary for him to shift his position in his chair to relieve the discomfort.

But something else had happened that night. The two of them had gone off to the party, and Cassie had changed. Joshua hadn't been able to figure out why, but the passion that had erupted in her earlier at the pond had cooled. Hell, it had frozen as solid as a glacier.

He'd tried to talk to her about it, but either the boys were always nearby or she was flying off on some pretense or another. He knew her little excursions were only ploys she used to avoid him. And she'd become very adept at those ploys over the past seven days.

So here he sat on this dreary Saturday morning with research to do and essays to read, yet he was helplessly focusing all his energies on Cassie.

As though his thinking of her conjured her image, she inched open his study door and entered. She obviously didn't know he was in the room because, without looking up, she went directly to the bookcase to her right, slid the book she had been carrying into its empty slot, and then turned back toward the door.

He watched her graceful movements and his gut wrenched. *Just let her go,* he told himself. She wasn't expecting a confrontation. But as she reached for the doorknob, his pent-up frustration refused to be silenced any longer.

"Cassie?"

Cassie's heart lurched in her chest and her gaze flew across the gloomy room to where Joshua sat behind his desk. "I thought you'd gone to the university." She could hear the accusation in her voice.

"As you can see," he said, "I'm right here."

"I was only putting back the dictionary I used last night."

"I've already given you permission to use the library."

He snapped on the reading light on his desk top and she could feel his intense eyes lock onto her like a tracking device designed to draw her nearer. There was a quarrel in the air, she could feel it.

Last Saturday night she'd decided to let Joshua know that a relationship between them was impossible, but she hadn't been able to bring herself to do it. She knew she'd have to invent a pack of lies to answer his inevitable questions and she just couldn't gather enough will to face the ordeal. Instead she'd simply stayed as far away from him as possible.

Since avoiding him had failed, she might as well relent to the conflict that crackled in the atmosphere. "I'm sorry I didn't knock," she said, her tone anything but apologetic. "But, like I said, I thought you'd left the house."

He stared silently for a moment before asking, "Cassie, how long is this going to go on? What's wrong?"

Her heart nearly broke at the hurt revealed in his question. But she couldn't let herself react to that. She had to focus on the cold, hard emotions, not the soft, tender ones.

"Nothing's wrong." *Lie number one,* she thought.

And her lie was like a sharp arrow that pierced him, she could see it from his pained expression.

"Please talk to me." He rested his elbow on the desk, his chin on his thumb. "We need to talk about what happened last weekend. We need to talk about us."

His eyes conveyed so much emotion, Cassie had to force herself not to look away. Anxiety rose inside her like fumes from a smoky fire that threatened to choke the life right out of her.

"But...the boys are waiting." *Lie number two.* But she conjured this deception with a hesitation in her raspy voice. Nevertheless the lie shot through the air, straight and true, landing with a wounding thunk.

"Maybe we can talk later," she said. *Lie number three.* Because if she had anything to do with it, they'd never discuss last Saturday night, they'd never talk about their relationship.

The distress evident in his dark eyes only added fuel to the flames of her apprehension. And the apprehension rose to panic level as she watched him stand, come around the desk and push the door closed. The latch clicked loudly in the silent room, and she felt cut off from the outside world.

"You will talk to me," he quietly demanded. "Right here. Right now."

She felt her eyes widen as she fought back the hysteria surging over her panic. What could she tell him? What lies could she use to make him—

The realization of what she was doing, what she was about to do, struck her like a stinging slap across the face. Lying to him only jeopardized her integrity. Lying only depleted her self-respect. Deceit was a mean and ugly thing.

But the truth would cost her everything.

As though deciphering her chaotic thoughts, Joshua said, "All I'm looking for are some honest answers."

At that moment the riot of anxiety inside her froze into a solid mass of fear. "I can't," she whispered, shaking her head.

"I want to know what happened between us. You're not leaving this room until you tell me what happened last weekend to make you—" his fingers grasped at empty air in frustration as he searched for a word "—change."

She understood exactly what he meant, he didn't need to explain. "Please." She felt her throat swell with emotion. "Don't make me tell you."

The golden flecks in his brown eyes glittered with determination. "I want to know. I *need* to know, Cassie."

The image of his face blurred when her eyes welled with tears.

"But it will cost me everything." She could barely get the words out.

The smallest frown of bewilderment creased his forehead, but the hardness never left his eyes. She could tell he was determined to push until he made his discovery.

Her heart beat so loudly she was certain he'd be able to hear its thump. She felt a sheen of perspiration break out above her lip and she wiped at it.

What she was about to tell him would change her whole life. She closed her eyes for the barest of moments before raising her lids to look directly into his gaze.

"We can't be together," she began shakily. "We can't date. We can't have . . . a relationship." She took a deep, trembling breath. "Other than that of your being Andy's father and my being Andy's nanny."

"But why?"

"Because we can't."

"Why?" His eyes narrowed and his nostrils flared.

"We just can't!"

He grabbed her upper arms. "Why can't we, Cassie?" The extent of his frustration was evident when he gave her a gentle shake. "I know you enjoyed being with me just as much as I enjoyed being with you. Tell me why?"

Sucking back a sob, she shouted, "Because I'm not good enough for you! I'm not worthy to have a relationship with someone like you. I'd never fit in with your friends!"

He released his hold on her. "What are you talking about?"

She looked at him, unable to hide her fear any longer.

"I never finished high school!" she blurted the hated words and then, shoving her way past him, she pulled open the door and ran from the room.

Chapter Nine

Joshua stood speechless at the door of his study and watched Cassie flee up the stairway. And even after she'd disappeared around the corner, he stood there.

If she had told him she was an alien from the planet Neptune, he wouldn't have been more surprised than he was at this moment.

She hadn't finished high school? How could something like that have happened to someone like Cassie?

He'd always imagined high school dropouts to be irresponsible juvenile delinquents or teenage, drug-addicted criminals—kids whose IQs matched their shoe sizes. Not someone as intelligent and perceptive as Cassie.

Finally he stepped back into his study and slowly closed the door. He stared at the floor, his hand still on the knob. Maybe she *did* have a tainted past.

Maybe she had been an unruly delinquent, a reckless and shortsighted—

No! His logical mind rebelled. Not the Cassie he'd come to know. Not the Cassie that he left in charge of his son every day. He wouldn't let himself believe it of her.

But, he wondered, did he not want to believe it because, if it were true, he'd then be guilty of neglecting his son by not checking out the woman he'd hired as his nanny?

Then another thought came to mind: maybe she did have a dark and shameful past, but she'd grown and matured into the trustworthy, fully capable woman he knew her to be.

He shook his head. The pieces of this puzzle didn't seem to fit. Or rather, he was missing a few of them.

Moving to his desk, he lowered himself into his swivel leather chair. He absently picked up the pencil and tapped it lightly against his chin as he tried to figure out exactly what he was going to do about this revelation of Cassie's.

Monday morning, Cassie came down to the kitchen feeling surprised all over again that she still had a job. Saturday afternoon when she'd confronted Joshua about whether he wanted her to leave his home, she'd experienced an odd mixture of relief and dark foreboding when he'd stated that he hadn't yet decided whether or not to dismiss her.

He'd acted extremely preoccupied the rest of the afternoon, and she'd felt on pins and needles, expecting him to up and fire her at any minute. But he hadn't.

Sunday had been her day off and she'd spent the day at the mall with Eric. They had eaten lunch out and gone to the movies. She stayed away from the house so Joshua could have some time alone with Andy.

She was actually glad it was Monday, the beginning of Joshua's work week. Pouring water into the coffeemaker, she switched on the machine to perk. As she slipped two slices of bread into the toaster, she noticed movement at the periphery of her vision. She glanced toward the door and saw Joshua standing there studying her. Her heart gave a great lurch at the sight of his handsome, clean-shaven face, and at the same time her stomach filled with a leaden sense of dread.

"Good morning," she murmured.

He gave her a curt nod but continued to stare, obviously mulling over some heavy thoughts. Cassie's self-consciousness got the better of her and she let her gaze slide to the floor.

The energy source that incessantly pulsed between them was as strong as ever, vibrating with a life of its own. But mingling with it this morning was an undulating tension that put Cassie in a frenzy. She needed to speak. She needed to break the silence that screamed between them.

"The coffee will be ready in just a minute or two," she said.

"Thanks, but I can't stay for breakfast." His voice sounded preoccupied. "I need to run."

She sensed rather than saw him take a couple of steps into the room.

"Andy and I missed Eric yesterday," he said. "Would you mind if next Sunday the three of us had a day out? You know, just the guys?"

Cassie stared at him speechless, realizing immediately what he was doing. Suddenly a lump formed in her throat at his attempt to assuage her fears about losing her job. He was letting her know that she and Eric would be here next week. What a wonderful man. She nibbled her bottom lip in an effort not to cry, and she nodded silently.

Then, in a tone hoarse with gratitude, she said, "Sure. Eric would love spending the day with you and Andy."

She felt she should say more. It was important to her to make him understand how much it meant to her to know that Eric had a real bed to sleep in, good, nourishing meals to eat, and a warm, secure house in which to live. But she simply couldn't voice the words right now without her emotions spilling down her cheeks in the form of tears, so she let it go, busying herself at the kitchen counter. She'd be certain to tell him later, when she had her wits about her.

Out of the corner of her eye, she saw him pace to the window and look out on the backyard. She knew he was giving her time to gather herself together. Wiping her hand across her face, she felt another rush of emotion, this one a deep sense of appreciation regarding Joshua's gentle treatment of her.

She admired his gallantry concerning the situation that she'd dropped in his lap this past weekend. He could have fired her on the spot. In fact, that's exactly what she'd expected him to do. Instead he'd spoken of the future—of taking the boys off together next weekend—in an effort to tell her she'd continue on as Andy's nanny. His actions made her tender feelings grow until she feared her heart wasn't big enough to contain all the love she felt for him.

Still, she couldn't help but wonder how he *really* felt about her terrible past. What did he think of her for being a high school dropout? She didn't dare ask. His answers might turn into talons capable of ripping and clawing at her full and vulnerable heart.

"Cassie." He turned to face her and she was relieved that she was able to look him directly in the eye.

"Before I leave for the day," he said, "I have something I want to tell you." Without waiting for a response, he continued. "Saturday, I called an acquaintance of mine. Doris is an administrator in the public education system. Andrew and I went to visit her yesterday, and she gave me some information about the state GED program."

Cassie went utterly still.

His tone dropped an octave and became very gentle as he said, "It's a general education program that will give you the opportunity to earn a certificate that's equivalent to a high school diplo—"

"I know what it is." Her nervousness forced the words to come out sharper than she'd meant for them to.

He pressed his lips together and looked at her a moment. Finally he rubbed his hand across the back of his neck and sighed. Then his determined gaze lifted once more to hers.

"The information is in the study. On my desk. We don't have to talk about it right now," he said. "Read over the literature today. Think about it. We can talk tonight.''

She couldn't read the expression in his dark, golden-flecked eyes. But when he made a wide berth around her to collect his briefcase and then walked out the door without another word, Cassie was overwhelmed by the deep sense of disgrace that descended on her like a thick fog. His tone, his coolly determined eyes, his very actions, spoke so loudly as to how his feelings toward her had changed.

It was as though she had actually turned into that fat, green, ugly toad—a *stupid* toad that he found repugnant and disgusting, so disgusting in fact that he didn't want to come too close.

She stood in the kitchen fighting back tears of humiliation. The sunlight that pierced through the window split into a thousand shining fragments as her eyes watered and stung.

Cassie had never meant for him to find out; she'd tried so hard to keep him from discovering her secret. Whenever her past had caught up with her in previous jobs, she'd been upset about being terminated, but she'd always left each employer with her pride intact, completely certain she'd given her all. Doing every job to the best of her ability had been her life's adage.

However, there were two things that were different in this situation. The first was that, even though Joshua knew her secret, he hadn't dismissed her. She wouldn't be leaving this job. Not right away, anyhow. And she'd be seeing and interacting with Joshua on a daily basis, each of them knowing just how much she was lacking.

The other difference in this circumstance was one of utmost importance: she loved Joshua. She cared what he thought of her. She cared more than words could express.

Walking away from Professor Joshua Kingston with her pride intact was going to be a near impossibility. Keeping this job, for Eric's sake, was all important. Yet she could easily imagine those brown eyes of Joshua's turning on her with a contemptuous gaze that would chisel away at her self-esteem until she had none left.

But he's offered a way to change that, a silent voice beckoned for attention. *Joshua offered a way to change your whole life.*

She glanced toward the study, and sharp, frozen icicles of apprehension stabbed at her. But she hadn't time to ponder the feeling before the boys bounded into the kitchen shouting for breakfast.

Cassie avoided Joshua's study all morning long. But it was such a blatant evasion that she began to feel embarrassed at her behavior.

She'd baked a double batch of oatmeal-raisin cookies, and then after cleaning up the mess, she just about forced Andy and Eric into playing hide-and-seek with her in the yard. Finally the boys did everything short of coming right out and asking her to go into the house so they could play together.

The realization that she was procrastinating struck her just as the back screen door latched with a click. Why was she putting off going into the study to read the literature Joshua had left for her?

Completely fed up with herself, she took a quick glance over her shoulder at the boys and headed straight for the study.

She eased herself into Joshua's chair, the burgundy leather soft and supple with age. The mysterious, thoroughly male scent that was his alone permeated the chair, the desk, the very air of the room. Just being where he worked at grading papers, reading and calculating research data, made her feel so very close to him.

Cassie smoothed her palms over the desk top, then along the arms of the chair. Closing her eyes, she covered her mouth and nose with her hands and inhaled, slowly, deeply.

Joshua. She could smell him. Could picture in her head his attractive, intelligent face. Could almost feel his warm skin touching her arms, his firm, moist lips kissing her throat, her jaw, her mouth.

Letting her head relax against the chair back, she tilted up her chin and trailed her fingers lightly down the sensitive skin under her jaw and down her neck. It was such an easy thing for her to travel back into her memory to the night of the party—the night of their impassioned moments by the pond. The time she had spent in his strong arms would be an exquisite remembrance she'd cherish the rest of her life. He had wanted her. She'd known it by the yearning she'd seen in his gaze, by the furious beating of his heart, by the granite hardness of his desire that had pressed so intimately against her thigh.

The vivid memory made her gasp in heated response. Her eyes flew open and her head jerked upright.

Joshua may have wanted her at one time. But that was before he'd really known who she was, what she really was. And, now that he did know, he certainly didn't feel the same about her.

Cradling her forehead in her fingertips, she stared with unseeing eyes at the pile of papers and books he'd left on the desk for her. There was nothing she could do about how Joshua felt. The realization made her feel hopeless.

With a dreary grayness weighing heavy on her emotions, she opened the information pamphlet and began to read about the GED program sponsored by the State of New Jersey. The classes she would need to take, she learned, would focus on math and language skills, science, history and a few other subjects. Passing the timed, day-long test would earn her a general education certificate.

The person who had given Joshua the information had included several books and a sample test. She opened the math book, spent some time slowly flipping through the pages, and was relieved to see that the skills were primarily basic.

She looked up when she heard the back door bang shut. The boys began rummaging in the kitchen.

"We can make our own lunch," Eric called out to her.

"Yeah," Andy chimed in. "And we won't make a mess."

Cassie couldn't help but smile at their budding independence before she dipped her head down and became once more immersed in the textbook.

She scanned the science book and felt her stomach tighten with doubt and apprehension at the thought of having to learn and memorize all these facts.

After a while she rubbed her strained eyes and moved on to the history text. Although she'd never heard of some of the names mentioned, she became fascinated by the chronological events that changed the world. She recognized the names of many of the wars, but had never known the reasons behind them.

Time ticked by and she stretched her neck to relieve a crick. A glance at the clock let her know that, surprisingly, more than two hours had passed since she'd first sat down to read.

Because she hadn't heard a peep from the boys since lunch, she left the study and went toward the back of the house to check on them.

The kitchen counter was cluttered with an open jar of mustard, a butter knife, the opened loaf of bread and some leftover slices of American cheese, now dried at the edges to a dark yellow.

"Won't make a mess, huh?" she grumbled wryly.

Pushing her way outside, she inhaled to give Eric and Andy a good talking to about cleaning up after themselves. But once out on the back-porch step, all she saw was an empty yard.

The garage door was open and she went there, although she didn't really expect the boys to be playing where she'd expressly forbidden them to.

She circled the garage, and then walked out toward the back of the large yard. There was no sign of the boys at the pool, its water a calm, clear blue. Stopping at the wrought-iron bench under the old oak tree, she scanned the grounds of the neighboring homes.

When she called the boy's names several times and didn't get an answer, the first stirrings of concern quivered in her stomach.

"The house," she murmured to herself. "Check the house."

She jogged back the way she had come and went inside.

"Andy?" she called as she ran up the staircase. "Eric?"

The bedrooms were empty. She checked her room and then Joshua's, just to be thorough. Her jaw tightened with alarm as she rushed down the steps and completed a systematic search of the rest of the house. Her concern quickly turned to fear.

Where could they be? she wondered. Her thoughts began to fly, dark and frantic. A thousand different situations intruded on her, each one more dangerous than the last.

She stood in the kitchen; the faint scent of mustard hung in the air. Should she call Joshua? No, she decided, the situation wasn't that dire...yet.

"They probably took a walk," she murmured aloud. She wondered if maybe Eric and Andy had called out their plans to her and she'd been too involved with the books and the GED paraphernalia to hear.

They were probably out somewhere thinking that she knew where they were, thinking that she knew they were safe.

That's it. That's got to be it, she tried to tell herself.

But what if they were in some kind of trouble? The question hung over her like a heavy nimbus cloud

ready to burst into a torrent of rain. Should she call
the police?

What if they'd been taken from the yard?

"That's enough!" she scolded herself. There was no
need to become irrational here. And there was no sign,
no evidence whatsoever that anything happened other
than the boys decided to take a walk, or go to the lo-
cal baseball field. She wondered where that field might
be.

Grabbing her car keys off the hook on the wall, she
bolted for the door.

Cassie drove around the block, and then made a
wider circle around the entire perimeter of the neighborhood. Her stomach jumped with fear and dread,
and her brain wouldn't stop conjuring those horrible
mental pictures. She'd never known she'd had such a
wild imagination. If she didn't find those boys soon,
she was going to go crazy!

On her third loop through the neighborhood, she
spotted a playground. Her heart sang with happiness
when she saw a group of boys playing baseball.

She parked the car, got out, and scanned the field.
Her elation quickly subsided when she didn't see her
boys, and then it dissolved altogether when she questioned the children and learned that Andy and Eric
hadn't been there.

"Andrew Kingston wouldn't be here," one boy
said. "He's not allowed to play with us."

The group of children resumed their game, and she
thought of how Eric and Andy would enjoy joining
them. Joshua had eased up enough on Andy's restrictions that he might soon allow Andy to come to the
playground.

"Maybe that will change soon," Cassie whispered, and she found herself smiling despite the worry knotting her insides.

Cassie could easily imagine the lyrical, lighthearted laughter of Eric and Andy on their way to play ball with the other kids of the neighborhood.

"If nothing terrible has happened to them," she murmured, a worried ache squeezing her heart painfully.

She opened the car door and heaved a sigh as she slid behind the wheel. There was nowhere else to search. A bleak cloud of dismay smothered her and, hoping that maybe the boys had arrived back at the house by now, she drove home.

A faint tang of mustard wafted toward her when she entered the kitchen from the back door. She'd have to clean up the mess that the boys had left.

She was tightening the lid on the mustard jar when she heard the front door open and close.

"Eric?" she called, rushing toward the front of the house. "Andy?" She stopped short when she rounded the corner into the large foyer and met Joshua.

"Cassie, what's wrong?"

The tender concern in his tone nearly made her burst into tears. But this was no time to let herself melt under pressure.

"I can't find the boys," she explained.

His brows drew together. "How long have they been gone?"

"At least two hours." She took her top lip between her teeth for a moment and then miserably confessed, "Maybe longer."

He didn't ask for an explanation, he didn't have to. His countenance alone was enough to make Cassie stammer out a confused mixture of apologies and excuses.

As Joshua watched the deep anguish on Cassie's face and heard sincere regret color her tone, his heart tightened so agonizingly that he could hardly focus on the words tumbling from her mouth.

Andrew and Eric were missing, that much he knew. But for the life of him, he couldn't make out how the GED program fit into all this.

He raised his hand to quiet her, and he was about to ask a few questions when that single moment of silence was interrupted with a loud crash coming from the garage.

"It sounds like they've come home," he said softly.

"Thank God!"

He followed Cassie through the hall to the kitchen and out to the garage. They rounded the corner, she a split second before him. Her gasp met his ears the same instant that his gaze fell on the boys—the mud-encrusted, dank-smelling boys.

"Are you all right?" he asked them.

Eric's chest puffed out proudly and he grinningly proclaimed, "We've had ourselves a Huck Finn adventure."

"Yeah, Dad," Andrew added, "we started building a fort over in the woods."

"Pierson's Woods?" Joshua heard the incredulity in his own voice. "That's nearly two miles from here."

"It feels like I walked about a thousand," Andrew said.

"Son, why would you go off without telling Cassie where you were going?"

"But we told you, Dad," Andrew said. "We were having an adventure."

"And," Eric added, "it wouldn't have been a Huck Finn adventure if anybody knew where we was."

"Where we *were*," Joshua corrected automatically, and he really had to quell his desire to chuckle at the boys' spunk. He could easily remember some of the daring adventures he'd had as a child.

But as he glanced over at Cassie's beautiful, pale face, concern knitting her brow, he knew he couldn't let his son or Eric get away with this little episode without punishment—no matter how much he might understand and empathize with their impetuous spirit.

"It was wrong of you boys to go off without telling Cassie," he began.

"But if we asked Cassie," Eric sputtered, "she'da said no."

"Of course I would have said no." Cassie stepped farther into the garage. "I don't even know where Pierson's Woods is, and—"

"See?" Eric said.

"Yes, I see. And that's precisely the point," Joshua calmly stated. "The two of you willingly and knowingly went off without Cassie's permission."

"But, Dad—"

"No buts." Joshua cut Andrew's lament to the quick with his sharp tone. "Neither one of you will leave this yard for two days. And there will be no television for a week."

"A week?" Andrew's eyes grew large.

His father's gaze narrowed and his voice grew utterly serious as he asked, "Would you like to go for two?"

The shoulders of both boys dropped, as did their gazes. "No, sir," they muttered in unison.

"Go strip off those dirty clothes," Joshua ordered. "And get yourselves showered and changed. Stay in your rooms until Cassie calls you for dinner. And both of you owe her an apology. She was worried sick about you."

"Sorry, Cassie," Andrew said.

"Sorry." Eric's voice was suddenly thick with emotion. "I didn't mean for you to be worried."

"Now, go and do as I told you," Joshua said. "Andrew, make certain that you take a dose of medicine from your inhaler. You sound wheezy."

"Just a little," Andrew mumbled grudgingly as he walked out the wide door.

The boys left behind a thick, tense silence, Joshua noticed as he looked over at Cassie.

"It's funny how kids are determined to get in the last word," he said, hoping to deionize the anxious energy in the air.

His eyes didn't miss the almost imperceptible tremble of her chin and he wanted badly to go to her, hold her and make her fears go away. But he didn't dare. He knew she wouldn't welcome or appreciate any comfort from him—not after the way she'd been acting toward him since he'd forced her to reveal what she obviously considered her awful secret.

She bit her bottom lip to stop its quivering. He watched her delicate throat muscles convulse and he was certain she was about to cry.

"Cassie, it's okay," he assured her gently. "The boys are safe."

It took her a moment to rein in her emotions, and even though he had a dozen things he wanted to say to her, he kept silent and gave her the time she needed.

Her chest rose with her inhalation, and when she finally spoke, the words were released fast and furiously. "But it isn't okay. Don't you see that? I should never have gone into the study. I avoided that part of the house all morning. I should never have sat down at your desk. Should never have opened that first book. I can't do this, Joshua. Don't you understand? I just can't!"

He simply stood there, watching her. He could easily see from the look on her face that she had more to say. And he was anxious to hear it.

"I can't be everything to everyone," she said. "I can't keep this job as Andy's nanny and raise Eric and go back to school. I simply can't do it all!"

"I'll help you." The words slipped from his mouth without thought.

"No!"

Although she didn't raise her voice, there was fury and something else in her tone—something he couldn't quite identify.

"You haven't been listening," she said. "If I hadn't been so involved with those books you left on your desk for me, I wouldn't have lost track of the boys. I shouldn't have been reading about the GED program. I wouldn't have—"

"But, Cassie, you heard what Eric and Andrew said," he told her. "They waited for you to become preoccupied. They didn't want to ask permission because they knew you wouldn't give it. They slipped away. On purpose. If you hadn't become distracted by the GED information, it would have been something else."

"No," she firmly disagreed. "That's not true. I'm good at my job. The boys would never have been able to—"

He couldn't help but laugh. "Cassie, you can't watch their every move. I don't expect—"

"But that's my job!"

There was an unrelenting quality in her words, in the set of her body, that somehow struck him wrong. There was more going on here than Cassie simply feeling responsible for having lost track of the boys. He wished he understood what was going on in her head. Maybe he could better unravel the mystery that was Cassie if he could get her to talk, get her to give him a little more information—information about her past.

Finally he very gently, very compassionately, asked her the question that had been burning inside him for days. "How did this happen?"

"But I told you," she said, near tears. "I became wrapped up with the books—"

"Not that," he interrupted with a shake of his head. "How in the world did you . . . ?" He felt at a loss for words, but then started again. "What happened to make you quit school?"

For a moment he was certain she would refuse to tell him. But then the story tumbled from her like water bursting from a strained dam.

He heard it all; the father who died unexpectedly, leaving no savings, no life insurance; a mother who lost interest in life itself; a brand-new baby brother who needed food, clothing, shelter, and money to buy all those things.

"So I quit high school," Cassie explained, now dry-eyed. "And found work."

"But weren't there state agencies to help you?"

"My mother made me believe that the state would take Eric." Her eyes were wide with an odd mixture of fear and determination, as though the horrible ordeal was continuing to take place. "She didn't care. She was too sick, too despondent to care." Cassie glanced toward the door and lowered her voice before continuing. "In fact, I think she hoped he would be taken off her hands. But I couldn't let that happen. Eric was a helpless baby. It wasn't his fault. He needed me to love him, to care for him." Her chin tipped up defiantly. "Nobody else did."

Joshua stared in awe at this beautiful, dark-haired woman standing before him. Cassie had unselfishly given up her formal education, really her whole young teenage life, so that Eric could be provided for. Her story explained so much.

Again, he felt the overwhelming urge to go to her, to hold her, reassure her, offer her his supporting strength. But again, he helplessly kept his distance, knowing she would rebuff him. So he granted her his verbal approval only.

"You did the right thing, Cassie," he told her. "But now it's time for you to do something for yourself. You can enroll in the GED pro—"

"No," she said sharply. "I can't."

"You seem to forget," he said, desperate to force her to see what was possible. "The boys will be starting school in a little over a week. You'll have all day to—"

"Joshua, I don't want to talk about this anymore." Her eyes were determined, her mouth set firm. "I need this job. Eric needs for me to keep this job. And I already told you, I can't be everything for everyone. I'm just not—not—competent enough to do it all."

He frowned. She looked as though she were about to fall completely apart.

Then it came to him, and as quickly as the realization entered his head, it simultaneously slipped from his lips. "You're afraid."

He stared at her until she averted her guilt-ridden gaze. The sudden fury he felt toward her took him off guard.

"You're afraid you'll fail." His proclamation was louder this time. "Refusing to try for your GED has nothing to do with your job here as Andrew's nanny. It has nothing to do with your raising Eric. You're simply afraid you can't do it."

His analytical mind silently told him that his anger was illogical, that now was the time for compassion and understanding. But for some reason he couldn't seem to listen to logic. Not now. Not when he was so outraged to discover that Cassie would give up before she even tried. She wasn't a coward, why would she act like one?

"A few days ago you told me there was no chance for us to pursue a relationship," he said, fighting hard not to let his anger get the best of him. "I didn't understand then. I didn't agree with you."

He crossed his arms over his chest and his voice became deadly calm. "But now that I know the truth, I think you're right." A derisive hiss forced its way between his teeth. "But I also think you'll be surprised to hear that the reason a relationship between us is impossible has nothing to do with some certificate you haven't earned or how uneducated you think you are. But it does have everything to do with your lack of self-esteem."

He raked his fingers through his hair. "The woman in my life would have to have enough self-confidence to seek and explore every avenue. To live life to the fullest. She'd have to have a pride and respect for herself that would demand my own."

Joshua's unflinching gaze captured her and refused to let her go until he'd spoken his mind.

"The woman I give my heart to," he said, "will need to feel that she deserves my love. And she'll have to have the self-assurance it would take to trust me with her heart—her love."

Chapter Ten

Joshua was somewhere between the blissful state of drowsy sleep and consciousness when he heard the creaking hinges of his bedroom door as it was slowly opened and then closed again. He was reluctant to open his heavy eyelids. Sleep had been elusive for the past several nights. Ever since he'd lost his temper and verbally battered Cassie.

He felt terrible about what he'd done. He felt even more terrible about the fact that he hadn't talked to her, apologized for the things he'd said. But every time he saw her, his anger and frustration seemed to flare anew, so he remained silent. This hostility was eating him up inside and he knew he should move beyond it, that he should—

His mattress shook as someone climbed onto it and Joshua finally opened his groggy eyes.

"Are you awake?"

The innocence in Andrew's whispered question tugged at Joshua's heartstrings. One corner of his mouth curled wryly.

"I sure am," Joshua whispered back. "Good morning."

Andrew lay down beside him, staring intently into his eyes. The serious expression on his son's face made him want to frown, but he forced himself not to. He could tell Andrew had something on his mind, something he wanted to discuss. But his fatherly instincts told him not to push, to let the boy lead the way in his own good time.

This heightened intuition he felt toward his son was all thanks to Cassie. He knew it just as surely as he knew the sun would rise in the east and set in the west. Of all the nannies he had ever hired for his son, Cassie was the only one who calmly and rationally talked to him about his son's needs as a growing boy. She had made him aware of his overprotective tendencies, and she'd done it in a way that hadn't made him feel inadequate about his parenting skills. He guessed she knew, through raising Eric, that parents have enough to feel guilty about without having to feel as though they have failed.

Cassie was a special person, kind, loving, caring. And bright. And it frustrated him no end that she didn't seem to see it.

Joshua pushed himself up in bed and rested his back against the headboard. Out of the corner of his eye, he saw Andrew mimic the action. Joshua lifted his arm and cradled the back of his head in the palm of his hand, and again, his son followed suit.

Reluctant to make Andrew feel belittled in any way, Joshua checked the warm-hearted smile that threatened to form on his lips. But he did allow himself the pleasure of gazing at his son and enjoying the tender emotions that pervaded every fiber of his being. God, how he loved this child.

"I'm worried," Andrew finally stated.

"About what, son?" he gently probed.

The boy sighed heavily, as though the weight of the world pressed on his shoulders.

"About Cassie," he said. "The last few days she's been walkin' around feelin' really bad. And she won't say why. It's like she's depressed or something."

Joshua's eyes widened and he cleared his throat so as not to chuckle at Andrew's shrewd, worldly-wise observation.

Finally Joshua sighed himself and admitted, "She probably is." He paused a moment, then went on. "You see, Cassie and I had words earlier in the week."

"You guys had a fight?"

"Well, not a fight exactly." Joshua couldn't bring himself to confess the terrible things he'd said to her. Andrew wouldn't understand. But then, when he thought about it, neither did he. Cassie's lack of education didn't change the person he knew her to be. A revelation seemed to hover on the fringes of his brain, but knowing his son was waiting for his response, he couldn't take the time to ponder it. "But I did say some things," he finally said, "that might have made Cassie feel..."

"Depressed?" Andrew supplied.

He nodded ruefully.

"You don't think she's gonna leave, do you?"

Joshua looked at his son's stricken countenance. "No," he assured. "I won't let that happen."

The determination he heard in his own voice provoked a sharp mental image; weeks ago he had promised Andrew he'd somehow convince Cassie to stay, and he had done so. Back then he'd acted on behalf of his son—giving Andrew the nanny he'd wanted had seemed all important at the time. Now, he realized, he wanted Cassie to stay just as much as Andrew did. More, even. Much more.

"'Cause you know," Andrew said, "Cassie is the best nanny who's ever watched me. She takes real good care of me *and* Eric. And she's real smart, too." His next words came out in a murmur, almost as though he contemplated them as he spoke. "Maybe somebody needs to tell her."

Joshua tilted his head to the side and simply stared at his son. "Out of the mouths of babes," he whispered.

"Huh?"

"Nothing, son." Joshua cast a bright smile Andrew's way. "You're pretty smart yourself."

He cocked a grin up at his dad. "I'm just a product of my environment."

Joshua laughed openly. "You certainly are." After a moment, he remarked, "You've become pretty fond of Cassie."

"She's nice," Andrew explained. "When I fell down and scraped my knee, she not only cleaned it and put some ointment on it, she gave me a cold washcloth for my face." He peered up into his dad's eyes, his voice lowering an octave as he bravely admitted, "I think she knew I was gonna cry. She plays ball with me and Eric. And she lets me have as much mustard on my sandwiches as I want." Then he wryly added, "As long as I clean up after myself."

"That's important," Joshua commented.

"And one of the best things I like—" again he cast a side-glance at his dad before continuing "—is when she tucks me in bed at night. She gives me a hug. Her hair smells all flowery. I love her." The last three words burst from him and his fair complexion flamed.

Joshua patted him on the knee. "It's okay if you love Cassie." He inhaled deeply and said, "In fact, I think that's what's wrong with me. I didn't know it until just now, but...I love Cassie, too. And I don't know what to do about it."

"Why don'tcha just tell her?"

Andrew's overly simplistic solution struck a chord in Joshua. Why didn't he just tell her? he wondered. He knew why.

"Well, after some of the things I said to her," he began his explanation slowly, "I'm not so sure telling her how I feel is such a good idea. I don't know how she'd respond."

"Were the things you said really mean?"

Joshua grimaced. "They weren't very nice."

"Wow," Andrew commented. "This *is* a problem."

They reclined on the bed, the only thing breaking the silence was the sound of the birds chirping outside the window.

"I know!" Andrew's voice was full of excitement. "I know what you can do, Dad. First off, ya gotta say you're sorry for hurting her feelings."

Joshua nodded. "I can do that."

"Then, you gotta butter her up. You know, say she's nice and smart and pretty. Stuff like that."

Pressing his lips together to suppress the chuckle bubbling inside him at his son's suggestion, Joshua could only nod.

"Then," Andrew said with a shrug, "tell her you love her."

Joshua looked into his son's shining eyes and felt sentimental moisture prickle his own. His heart swelled with love until it was near to bursting.

"I'll do it," he announced around the lump that had formed in his throat. "I'll tell her how I feel."

"Great!"

Then a thought dampened his enthusiasm. "But I may have to wait. Today's Cassie's day off and she might have plans to go out."

"She might not, though," Andrew opined. "We were gonna take Eric to the park with us today. Why don't we ask Cassie to go, too?"

A slow smile crept across Joshua's mouth. "That's a great idea."

"I'm gonna go get dressed." Andrew hopped off the bed and hurried toward the door. "You get up, too, okay?"

"Right away." Then, when his son had opened the door, Joshua called out, "Hey, Andrew." Their gazes met affectionately. "Thanks, buddy," Joshua said.

Andrew gave him the thumbs-up sign before scampering out of sight.

Joshua sat up in the bed, stretching his shoulder muscles this way, then that. *Maybe somebody needs to tell her.* Andrew's words came into his mind with clear, childlike insistence.

Maybe Cassie *didn't* know how competent, how bright, how smart everyone thought she was. Maybe the self-assuredness she had shown on their first meeting—the composed, clearly capable ego that had convinced him to hire her—had been a facade, a mask she used to hide her vulnerability.

Remembering the downcast eyes, the rounded shoulders of defeat she had shown him earlier in the week, he knew the cocky, confident nature she'd evinced to get the job *had* been false.

He balled his fists, feeling the frustration once again filling him.

She was competent. And bright. And smart. Damn it all! And he would make her understand that. He was determined to make her see what a wonderful person she was.

Not too much later, Joshua walked into the kitchen, and smack into the middle of a fervent conversation between Andrew, Eric, and Cassie.

"I'm sorry, Andy," Cassie said. "But I can't go. I'm sure your father wouldn't want me intruding on the one day a week he gets to spend with you." She put two glasses of orange juice in front of the boys and turned back to the counter. "It's bad enough that he's going to be troubled with Eric—"

"But I'm no trouble," Eric said, affronted.

"Yeah," Andrew chimed in. "Eric's no trouble."

"I agree." Joshua took his cue. "He's no trouble at all."

Cassie whirled around, nearly dropping the serrated knife she was using to slice the bagels.

"I didn't know you had come down," she said.

Her words sounded breathless and beautiful to his ears. Now that Andrew had helped him to realize how he felt, the house looked brighter, the whole world sunnier. But nothing could surpass the beauty of the woman standing before him. He simply *had* to convince her to spend the day with him.

"Cassie, the boys and I would both like to have you join us at the park today," he said.

"But—"

"Please," he interrupted her.

Cassie looked into his strong, handsome face and she had to tighten her grip on the handle of the knife to keep her fingers from trembling. Her knees felt weak just standing in his presence.

Since their argument several days ago, she'd felt so hurt and humiliated by the words he'd flung at her that she'd avoided him. It hadn't been difficult. He'd spent a great deal of time at the university, and when he *was* home, he'd stayed holed up in his study.

But here he was proclaiming to want her to go with him on what should be her day off. She couldn't help wondering why. Did he have the notion to rail at her, to berate her some more?

As she gazed at him, though, she noticed that there was something in his eyes. Something in his face, in the tone of his voice, that she'd never seen or heard before. She had no idea what it was. Or what it meant.

"If you have nothing else planned," he added gently.

"No," she heard herself admitting quietly. "I'm not doing anything special."

"Then come with us."

He followed up his invitation with the most dazzling smile she'd ever seen—a smile that actually made
her feel weak in the knees. How could she possibly re-
sist?

"Okay," she said, but it sounded to her ears as
though the word had come from someone else, someone far away.

Cassie sat on the blanket with her feet tucked un-
derneath her and watched Joshua throw the baseball
first to Eric, then to Andy. She tugged at the waist
knot of her sleeveless white blouse, feeling utterly
confused.

What was she doing here? The question had echoed in her head the whole time she'd packed the pic-
nic basket and during the drive to the park that
surrounded Stringer's Pond.

Feeling jittery inside, she got up, absently smoothed
her palms over the back of her twill shorts, and headed
off toward the swings.

Joshua had been so right when he'd blatantly exposed her fear of failure. She hadn't even realized it
herself until she'd heard him say the words aloud. She
felt tears burning her eyelids and she dashed at them
with the back of her hand.

Earning her equivalency diploma had been something she'd always planned on doing. It had been her
unfulfilled dream. But there had never been time to do
it. She'd been so busy with Eric, with bills, with
money, with this job or that. She'd always been so
busy with life!

Easing herself down onto the swing, she lifted her feet and let the natural force of gravity gently rock her back and forth.

She didn't know how it had happened, but time had simply slipped by. And with each passing month, each passing year, the education she so desperately wanted seemed to drift farther and farther from her reach. And now, more than eight years after she should have earned her high school diploma, she *was* frightened that she might fail.

To fail the one thing she so badly wanted would be the ultimate humiliation. No, she thought, dipping her gaze to the ground and inhaling deeply to hold back the panic—failing *would* be horrible, but knowing that the man you loved thought you were a failure... now, that would be the worst. That would be unbearable.

But Joshua already knows that you're afraid to try. The silent, heart-wrenching words mocked her viciously. *That makes you a failure.*

"Cassie."

Lifting her face, she saw him standing in front of her. The gentleness in his voice, in his dark, attractive eyes, nearly made her cry. But instead she pressed her lips together and raised her brows in a querying manner.

"The three of us had fun playing catch." One corner of his mouth hitched up in a smile. "I wish you'd have felt like joining us."

Unable to get her larynx to work properly, she put on an apologetic countenance and shrugged one shoulder a fraction.

"The boys were getting hungry," he said softly, tenderly. "I told them to set up lunch and I'd come over and get you."

The sympathy she heard in his tone killed her. His anger had turned into empathy. That's why he'd invited her today, and that was why he was being so gentle and sweet right now. The last thing she wanted from Professor Joshua Kingston was his pity!

Tilting up her chin, she suddenly said, "Joshua, I'd like for you to find Andy another nanny. I think, with the way things are between you and me, that it would be best if I leave your house as soon as possible."

He looked stunned.

"Oh, I'll stay until you find someone," she assured him.

Joshua studied Cassie; her dark hair tumbling softly over her shoulders, her blue, blue eyes wide with single-minded determination, her slightly parted, coral lips. He felt that if he couldn't reach out and touch her peachy skin he'd die. But now wasn't the time.

He couldn't seem to get his wits together. He knew he should be arguing with her, asking—no, pleading—for her to stay, but none of the words that ran through his head seemed meaningful enough.

Apologize for the mean things you said, Andrew's little-boy voice announced silently in Joshua's brain, and before he could think about it, he found himself responding.

"Cassie, I'm sorry for the things I said to you."

A frown of uncertainty gathered between her neat, dark brows.

"I spoke out of turn about your education," he continued. "I'd like to ask you to forgive me. I'd like for you to stay on as Andrew's nanny. You've come to mean a lot to him." *And to me,* he thought, but couldn't bring himself to say it just yet.

"I'm happy Andy likes having me around," she said. "I love him as much as I love Eric. But, Joshua, the fact that I didn't finish my high school education is a big issue between us." She laughed ruefully. "I mean, look how we've acted all week. Barely saying two words to one another. You can't live like that. And besides, everything you said to me, hurtful or not, was the absolute truth."

"But I shouldn't have said them." His tone resonated with self-reproach.

They looked at each other through a thick fog of tension.

Finally, Andrew's voice echoed again in his head. *Butter her up,* it told him. *Tell her she's smart and nice and pretty.*

"You know," he started out slowly, "you're smart enough . . . just the way you are."

She made a humorless sound of incredulity. "Do you hear what you're saying? You, a college professor, are telling me that it's okay that I dropped out of high school. Come on, Joshua."

A stress-filled exhalation burst from him.

"That's not what I meant, damn it!" He grasped the steel chain of the swing. "Besides, I should never have butted my nose into your business. I should never have brought home the GED information. All I succeeded in doing was to make you feel bad about yourself." He raked his fingers through his hair in frustration. "Cassie, I don't care whether or not you have a high school diploma."

"Of course you care," she argued. "I spend all day with your son. Me, an uneducated, uncultured—"

"You are not uncultured!" The anger that burst from him was surprising, and he took a moment to calm down before adding, "I will not allow you to put yourself down like that."

She was staring at the bare earth under her feet and he reached out and tipped up her chin. "Cassie," he began gently, "you may not have earned your diploma, but a piece of paper cannot determine a person's worth."

"It helps," she snapped.

He simply stared at her. "You have no idea, do you?" he asked, his voice taking on an unusual quality that elicited her full attention. "You have no inkling of what you have done for me. As a father, I mean. You, the uneducated person that you are," he parroted her words at her to make a point, "have taught me that there's more to being a parent than guarding your child against harm, that it's also letting go. You've improved my relationship with Andrew two hundredfold. And the change in Andrew is remarkable. Just look—"

"Cassie! Cassie!"

Eric's terrified voice immediately drew their attention.

"My God," Joshua whispered. "What's wrong with Andrew?"

They sprinted across the grass and Joshua reached the blanket first. Andrew looked lethargic. Joshua noticed how his son's lips were tinged blue.

"What happened?" Panic caused Joshua to shout the question at Eric.

The boy's chin quivered, then words rushed from his mouth. "We were havin' a contest to see who could take the biggest bite of sandwich. We were laughin' and jokin' around."

Cassie sat down.

"Can you breathe?" she calmly asked Andrew.

"When he started acting funny," Eric continued, although the adults no longer paid attention, "I thought he was just foolin'."

"He's choking." Joshua smacked his son sharply between the shoulder blades.

"Joshua, no!" Cassie yelled. "That will only cause what's in his throat to lodge there."

She pushed Joshua out of the way and positioned herself behind Andy. With one fist balled, she placed her hands at his solar plexus and gave several sharp, upward thrusts. Joshua could only watch, horrified.

The crust of bread flew from between Andrew's lips, and he instantly took a deep, ragged breath. Then he gave in to a bout of coughing before again inhaling deeply.

After several moments Cassie asked him, "You okay, now?"

Andrew nodded, intent on getting air into his lungs.

Cassie could actually see the relief flood through Joshua. He was such a good and loving father. She only wished he truly believed what he'd said to her a few minutes ago, that a diploma couldn't prove a person's worth.

"Are you sure you're okay?" he asked, hugging his son tightly.

"Yeah." Andrew squirmed in his embrace. "Daaaad," he complained.

The suspenseful incident seemed to rob everyone of their appetite. But when Joshua asked if the boys would like to go home, the answer was a unanimous "No!"

"Could we go climb the monkey bars?" Andrew asked.

"You sure you're up to it? Maybe we should see the doctor."

Andrew rolled his eyes heavenward. Cassie had to laugh at this blatant sign of sufferage.

"Okay. Okay," Joshua relented. "Go play."

Cassie watched the boys scamper off toward the playground.

"I don't know how to thank you."

She turned her gaze on Joshua.

"You saved his life, you know."

"I wouldn't go that far," she said.

"The way I was pounding on him?"

Cassie shrugged, not knowing what to say.

He slid closer to her and took her hands in his, the feel of his skin against hers deliciously warm even on this sunny day.

"Cassie, if this doesn't show you just how much you're worth," he said, his voice quiet with utter sincerity, "then nothing ever will."

He gently squeezed her fingers. "I mean, look at you. You dropped out of school to provide for a sick mother and a baby brother. You continued to provide, even after your mother died and you were left sole guardian of Eric. *And you survived.* That's success. That's achievement."

She searched his gaze, knowing that everything he said was true. But she'd never had anyone actually say the words out loud. Well, Mary had, but Cassie just hadn't been convinced. However, here was a scholarly man, a highly intelligent man, telling her she was a success. She found it overwhelming.

"Cassie," he continued, "education isn't all books and essays and diplomas. It's a constant process. Education has to do with learning new things. You've continued your education. You learned to swim so you could work as a lifeguard. You took a first-aid course. And you're constantly using the books in my library to look up one thing or another. Cassie, you've been furthering your education without even realizing it."

He meant the words he was saying. She could tell from the intensity of his dark, golden-flecked eyes. And it made her feel *wonderful!*

"I didn't bring you the GED information because *I* thought you needed it." He raised his hand to cup her cheek. "I brought it because *you* thought you needed it. You feel somehow deficient or inferior because you haven't earned your diploma. But you're neither of those things."

She tried to avert her gaze, but he refused to let her.

"Cassie, you can do it," he said. "You can easily earn your GED certificate." He grinned. "It'd be a cinch with me as your coach."

"I don't know," she whispered.

"I know you're afraid. That's normal."

With doubts continuing to tarry, she said, "But it's important to me to do a good job as Andy's nanny."

"Then, don't do it as Andy's nanny. You're fired."

Before she had time to even feel shocked, he added, "Do it as my wife."

He cradled her face between his palms and heard his son's final piece of advice echo in his head. *Tell her you love her.*

"You see," he told her, "I love you, Cassie. And whether you earn your certificate or not, I'm going to continue to love you."

His words actually startled her. She reached up and encircled his wrists with her fingers and asked, "What did you say?"

His voice grew husky and low as he said, "I said, whether you earn your certifi—"

"No, no." She felt breathless and giddy with joy. "The other part."

He looked at her a long moment. "I said, I love you."

"But—b-but," she stammered, her heart pounding furiously, "you said a relationship between us was impos—"

"Forget what I said." His eyes twinkled in the sunlight. "I was stupid."

He loved her. He loved her! Cassie could hardly believe it.

Her smile grew sultry, lingering. "You, stupid? Never. Your intelligence is the sexiest thing about you."

"Sexy, huh? Are you telling me you feel something for me that I should know about?"

"I'm telling you that I love you, too."

He kissed her then, lightly on the mouth.

"Oo-oo," he groaned. "If we weren't in public..."

Then she kissed him. One teasing, tender kiss on the palm of his hand and another on his chin.

"Tell me," she implored. "Tell me what would happen if we were in private."

"I'd kiss you," he said. "I'd kiss you until you couldn't breathe. And none of these chaste, for-everyone-to-see kisses, either." His tone lowered. "They'd be hot." Then he whispered, "And wet. And they'd last deep into the night."

Now it was her turn to groan. "Tell me more."

"I'd touch you," he said softly. "I'd run my fingers through your silky hair. And over your velvety skin. And I'd taste your honeyed sweetness from here—" his thumb lightly grazed the hollow of her throat "—to here." He traced a slow, sensuous trail to the tender underside of her chin.

"Oh, stop!" She chuckled deliciously. "The thought alone is killing me."

He exhaled a long-suffering sigh. "But for now, I'll have to settle for a modest, passionless kiss."

She stopped him before their lips met, gazing at him with ardent eyes. "Modest, maybe," she told him. "But never passionless."

And then she let him cover her mouth with his.

Across the playground, Eric's eyes grew wide when he caught sight of Joshua and his sister.

"Yuck," he said, his voice full of the kind of disgust only an eight-year-old could muster. "They're kissin'!"

"All right." Andy came to stand beside Eric. "That means he told her."

"Told her what?" Eric's face was still scrunched up.

"That he loves her," Andy announced.

Eric took a moment to digest this information. Finally he turned to Andy. "Do you think they'll get married?"

"They're kissin', aren't they?"

A happy grin split Eric's face. "We'll be stepbrothers. Great!"

"Well, Cassie's your sister. If she marries my dad . . ." Andy stopped to think.

"I'll be your uncle!" Eric exclaimed.

Andy laughed. "Cool!"

They congratulated each other by slapping a high-five. And then they turned back to conquer the monkey bars.

* * * * *

Get Ready to be Swept Away by
Silhouette's Spring Collection

Abduction
& Seduction

These passion-filled stories explore both the dangerous
desires of men and the seductive powers of women.
Written by three of our most celebrated authors, they are
sure to capture your hearts.

Diana Palmer
Brings us a spin-off of her Long, Tall Texans series

Joan Johnston
Crafts a beguiling Western romance

Rebecca Brandewyne
New York Times bestselling author
makes a smashing contemporary debut

Available in March at your favorite retail outlet.

MILLION DOLLAR SWEEPSTAKES (III)

is
DIANA PALMER'S
THAT BURKE MAN

He's rugged, lean and determined. He's a
Long, Tall Texan. His name is Burke, and he's
March's *Man of the Month*—Silhouette Desire's
75th!

Meet this sexy cowboy in Diana Palmer's
THAT BURKE MAN, available in March 1995!

Man of the Month...only from Silhouette Desire!

Arriving in April from Silhouette Romance...

Bundles of JOY

Six bouncing babies. Six unforgettable love stories.

Join Silhouette Romance as we present these heartwarming tales
featuring the joy that only a baby can bring!

THE DADDY PROJECT by Suzanne Carey
THE COWBOY, THE BABY AND THE RUNAWAY BRIDE
by Lindsay Longford
LULLABY AND GOODNIGHT by Sandra Steffen
ADAM'S VOW by Karen Rose Smith
BABIES INC. by Pat Montana
HAZARDOUS HUSBAND by Christine Scott

Don't miss out on these BUNDLES OF JOY—only from Silhouette Romance.
Because sometimes, the smallest packages can lead to the biggest surprises!

And be sure to look for additional BUNDLES OF JOY
titles in the months to come.

BOJ1